Mannequin

A novel

Stefan Plesoianu

Previous works: *Thorn – a contemporary novel*

Cover design: Lucia Motoc
Find her work on Instagram at: lucia.motoc

"God didn't need to send us hangmen, there are only so many nights without tears...at the dawn of life tremble the shadows of death. Isn't light but a hallucination of the night?"

- Emil Cioran

Chapter I

It terrified me to know that at some point I would lose my mind. Nothing justified that fear, but one incident did confirm my suspicion, however. The death of my mother came as such a shock that I simply could not get over it. And amid that unimaginable pain, even if temporarily, I wound up in a state which can only be described as insanity. In a way, I stayed in that zone ever since. It's absurd how the world goes on like nothing happened, oblivious to people's tragedies. After all, it's normal that some people end up crazy.

A pleasant wind brushed gently against my skin as if I floated in a dream. I'd had a surreal sensation throughout most of my life, in fact, so the wind only added to it. Across the street, the shop I inherited from my family, which earned me a subsistence level income without me having to do much; behind me, the apartment block where I lived, with numerous minuscule dark spots scattered on its surface. Shining in the soft, yellow light of the street lamps, cockroaches crawled lazily, looking for each other or searching for passages into the flats of my neighbors. My entire life took place in that perimeter. Every now and then a light turned on in the building, stopping the nearby roaches in their path for a few seconds. Since it was late at night, the light didn't last long, just enough for a person to start hunting down a mosquito and then give up and go back to bed, so the cockroaches quickly resumed their swarm.

A faint rumble came from the distance. It steadily intensified until a black Audi shaped up and eventually stopped in front of me.

"Alright, let's get this done. I banged my shoulder earlier, so you're gonna have to do the digging. They handed him to me in one piece, but we can easily roll him out of the trunk; there's no way I lift anything tonight."

Bone and I had been partners for a couple of years already, during which we buried two bodies together. Even though this was barely my third 'cleaning' job, it felt normal to me, as if I'd been doing it my whole life. While Bone had become involved in many operations and sometimes did more than just the 'cleaning', I only came in at the end to help him out. When he initially proposed to link up, he was still down the pecking order in his entourage, so the lowly tasks, such as disposing of the leftovers, were given to him. He did, however, have the freedom to not work alone. We'd been friends since high school, though we were never close or anything. We merely happened to get along well and he somehow got the impression I wouldn't mind getting involved in a side hustle like this, as long as I didn't have contact with his superiors and my hands remained clean, in theory.

"Your gift will have to wait a bit, by the way. I'll come by and drop it as soon as I get my own piece, so don't worry about it," Bone said.

Disposing of bodies paid pretty well, especially since it wasn't a particularly difficult job. Nor dangerous, for that matter, as long as I limited my commitments to that. Besides, it obviously made no sense for me to betray Bone's trust since his bosses surely knew about me and could easily get rid of me if I caused them problems.

"How's Bella doing?" I asked him.

"Ugh," he sighed. "It doesn't matter I'm bringing major dough in, or that we can suddenly afford all these nice things, she's on my case every time I put in a night shift. I get home in the morning dead tired, all I want is to pass out on my bed and catch a break. But she's thinking about having a kid lately, so she's afraid of something happening to me, to us. I don't know why she gets so pissed about it, I told her I'm doing safer stuff now."

"She loves you, man. You're lucky to have her."

"Yeah, I know. The only thing I'm missing right now is sleep."

The car made a left turn and got off the paved road onto a forest track. We were heading to a small valley in the woods, about ten minutes away from the edge of the forest. We lived in a quaint old town, not exactly brimming with life yet not deserted either. Some time ago it used to be an important location, now being more of a nexus for the arteries connecting the important cities in the country. Nature unfolded itself along the periphery of our town with forests, hills, and gorges, carved by the river Aries. A tiny patch of humanity dropped in the middle of the wilderness, we were an ideal location for shipments of bodies and other incriminatory evidence from neighboring places, such as our companion in the trunk.

"I'm really surprised how cold Bella is, to be honest," Bone went on. "Like, she knows the stuff I currently do, she knows I'm climbin' the ladder and pullin' off bigger moves now, but still nags me about it. Yet, if she was here with us in the car, I bet she wouldn't even flinch if we told her about our buddy in the back."

"She's an ice cube wrapped in a marshmallow," I said. Then the car hit a bump and a clunking sound came from the back.

"You sure he croaked? I can dig a hole, but don't feel like popping my cherry tonight," I told Bone.

"Nah, we're good. Honestly, for what they pumped in him, if he's still alive he deserves to walk away freely."

It's not like I had an affinity for that sort of business, for violence or any criminal stuff whatsoever. Or as if having a murderous mobster friend did anything for me, such as empowering me or making me feel cool or important. Frankly, the sole reason I did what I did was that it made no sense not to do it. Merely a passenger in my own life, nothing held me back from helping Bone out, as long as I felt warmly about him as a friend and as long as I knew everything would go on the same without me – the same people would get in the way of Bone's bosses, get clipped and be driven to the exact same valley to be laid to rest, by Bone alone or helped by someone else other than me. It generally made no difference for anyone or anything that I did what I did, so it made no difference for me either.

Bone stopped the car, turned off the lights, picked up a lantern, and got out. He wore an all-black, loose outfit with a fine silver chain around his neck, a four-year anniversary gift from his girlfriend. Seeing him stand up made me aware of his height; well-built and quite tall, I only now took notice of it for the first time, since I was slightly taller than him.

"Ah, damn it, I might have to get it checked out," Bone grabbed his shoulder while inspecting the surroundings. "This will have to do," he said pointing me where to dig. "Whenever you feel like it, just let's not make it too late."

It took me a fair while to make any real progress. Digging a hole meant tiresome work, especially since I did it alone. The first layers of dirt contained many squirming insects and worms, disturbed in the silence of the night by my shovel and Bone's lantern. The deeper I dug, the wetter and harder the dirt got. I noticed Bone was getting cold on the side, smoking his third cigarette already.

"It's not two meters deep yet, but it could work. What do you think?" I asked him, knowing he wanted to go home and sleep.

"Uhm, I don't know...Yeah, screw it, it is what it is. No one's gonna smell it around here."

He helped me out of the hole, then we headed to the trunk. Kept inside a black bag, Bone grabbed the body by the head, while I grabbed the feet. We rolled it out, then all the way to the hole.

"Stripped or wrapped?" I asked.

"It's pretty cold in the woods this time of year, so it'll take it a while to decompose. We gotta strip him."

Bone ripped open the trash bag. The cadaver's eyes were still open, staring bleakly into the night.

"What did he do?"

"He overstepped his mark, let's leave it at that," Bone answered me.

The sight of corpses had no effect on me, weirdly

enough. No negative effect, to be precise, as the first time I helped Bone clean and saw a dead body, it calmed me profoundly. Having this much close contact with death, of the finite passed over into eternity, silenced all the worries, insecurities, and anxieties of life. Not so much an answer to the questions, as much as those questions being erased forever. Fair to say I didn't want to die, but being dead represented an alleviating thought, definitively cemented by the sight of the corpses I buried.

We stripped him down to his underwear, then pushed him into the hole.

"Alright, I'mma light up the clothes then we can go," he said.

"Here?"

"No, in my kitchen once I get home. Yeah, of course here."

"Do it on the tracks at least, or throw them down and burn everything all together. Don't harm the forest, man."

So we did. I got down in the hole with the body, which bore a strikingly indifferent look on its face with regards to what was happening to it. I burned the clothes, filled up the grave and we left. The drive home was smooth, the car glided through the thick night piercing it with its lights, not unlike a submarine flowing through the deep ocean.

Bone told me again how he recently received a

promotion, climbing the ranks and closing in on the bigger fish in the pond, something difficult to achieve given he still lived in our hometown. He also tested the water with me, I sensed, mentioning how increasingly difficult it became for his crew to ply their trade, how many middlemen quit over the rising number of police interventions, expanded surveillance and, of course, the exigent demands of the mobsters. All of this was to let me know that he might need me for additional operations in the future, perhaps in another capacity too, other than associate cleaner. I let him talk, pondering whether there were any ways I could end up being forced to do it, as I had no interest in it. For the time being, at least, Bone and I were more buddies rather than partners, so I needn't think about that yet.

Bone dropped me off in front of my apartment building.

"That's all she wrote for today. Thanks, Chrissy, I owe you for the digging. I'll come by as soon as I have the cash."

"No probs. How about you spice up that envelope a bit though, for the extras tonight?" I joked.

"I'll throw half of bone more for the sake of friendship. We good?"

"I didn't really mean it, but I wouldn't mind. It's up to you."

A bone meant three hundred bucks. It was just a

little word play we did, to make the financial aspect a bit amicable.

"You good at shooting?" he asked me prior to starting the engine.

"I never fired a gun. Why are you asking?"

"Just thought a little practice wouldn't do any harm. In case shit goes down, you see. I know you're not up for that kind of mission, but still. It could be fun anyway."

"It's not exactly my kind of fun..."

"Here's the thing, I snaked a couple of mannequins from this hall last week. They'd make great targets for practicing. You know what, I'll pick you up in a couple of days, just try it out and see if you like it."

He started the car and flicked the cigarette out the window.

"Alright Boney, we'll see how it goes. Say hi to Bella for me, will ya?"

"She says hi back," Bone grinned and drove off.

My problems with nightmares started early in my childhood. Originally, I was scared of the dark, which is why I shared a bed with my mother for longer than normal, if that's even normal at all. I've heard that the mother is meant to nurture and provide shelter, and the father to open the child's eyes to the outside world, so since I grew up fatherless it was probably the reason I didn't like sleeping alone. Once my mom emigrated to her own bed, I had problems falling asleep, imagining all sorts of things in the dark until exhaustion overcame me.

Simultaneously, the nightmares started. After a few years, fed up with my fear of the dark, I locked myself up in the bathroom at night with the light turned off, forcing myself to face my issue. Slowly, I managed to control it, and falling asleep became easier. The nightmares continued without relent, however, right until I buried my first corpse. During adolescence, my terror partially morphed into anger, which kept building up in parallel to the nightmares. Witnessing death so closely cured me of both, similar to exposure therapy. Probably it showed me how easily anger and fear came to an end, and how little they actually meant.

Life breezed by relatively uneventfully for the past two years, apart from the missions with Bone. Besides him, I also had Mrs. Trent, a kind, caring old lady. She and I became close after I moved in since we were the least odd ones in our building. I didn't know exactly what my other neighbors did for a living, although I would have guessed that the couple on the first floor did homemade porn, based on the lights in their room, the strange noises late at night and the stuff they bought from my store. I barely had any contact with anyone in that building apart from Mrs. Trent, who'd taught literature at a university in France, had traveled a lot, and was obviously well-educated and soft-spoken. One of the four apartments on the second floor where we lived had a lock on the door, no one knew why, but it'd always been like that apparently. I lived right opposite Mrs. Trent; her door still had the initial silver letter used to number the apartments. Mine had fallen off and I didn't bother to replace it.

I entered the building and made my way to the apartment. When the automatic light turned on, a single cockroach froze motionless, while the others were nowhere to be seen. They were smarter than to hang out in the open; instead, you could find scores of them piling under the rain gutters and in the basement. The entire town had them, there wasn't much that could be done about the infestation. I stepped on the roach and then kicked it towards the entrance. Climbing up, my floor seemed clear. I got into my apartment, consisting of a large living room, modestly furnished, with an open kitchen, a bedroom, a tiny storeroom, a bathroom, and a balcony towards the street.

It was Saturday night and I could sleep in if I wanted since my manager normally took the Sunday shifts at the store. We mainly sold food and some basic cleaning products, although we had a small selection of cigarettes and alcoholic drinks too. My manager, Kim, worked full-time making orders and checking that every product had the correct price tag under it, as well as putting them on the right shelves.

The other person on my payroll, George, the salesman, was an honest young man living three minutes away from the store. They switched between them behind the counter, with Kim earning more than George for her dual role, of course. As I said, the store only earned me a subsistence level income although, given my simple lifestyle and subsequent lack of expenses, it combined nicely with the 'cleaning' fees.

Ultimately, perhaps the only thing which still gave me some sort of joy: by the closed balcony door, positioned carefully to absorb the very first rays of sunlight, my four peach seedlings, planted as pips and now thinly, steadily stretching upwards. The brittle stems rose simultaneously from their baby pots, each twisting in a different direction from the next. Although the four pits came from the same species of fruit, every set of leaves differed in shape and orientation from the others; my peaches were all unique, though were raised in the same soil, behind the same window, and with the same love.

And so the time passed, observing new baby leaves grow, going to the store, melding one day into the next, and holding on to peace and quiet. Yet simultaneously, a hidden discontent brewed in me as I waited for something to happen to disrupt this secretly unbearable harmony.

Chapter II

I waited for Bone in front of my building, soaking up the sun. A brief but powerful shower followed the storm from the previous day, so the pavement hadn't had time to dry up yet after the cold night. The wind halted for a while, just enough for the trees to catch a break and the people to walk around dressed slightly more casually.

Watching Bone's car turn a corner, then steadily shape up as it approached became almost a ritual. When the car stopped in front of me, I went around and got in.

"Ready to pop some caps?" he asked with a grin.

"Let's see how it goes. You stole some mannequins you said? That's such a random thing to do."

"Well, it's done now, so it doesn't matter. I don't know, I suppose I'm an opportunist, what can I say?"

It appeared Bone more often than not carried something in the trunk of his car, usually illicitly too. Even though the car was merely five years old (the previous owner bought it new, though Bone found a way to make him sell it a year later for a fraction of the price), it had already traveled a significant distance. Bone considered buying a new one if given the opportunity to do it cheaply, of course, for personal use, and keep the Audi as a work car.

"Bella said you should join us for dinner one of these days. She misses your face, she said. I don't see how that could be possible if you ask me," he poked fun.

"Well since she doesn't mind seeing yours every day, anything is possible," I hit back.

The joyous beam on his face rolled back the years; whenever he joked, he had the same lightness about him as he did ten, fifteen years before. I hoped he would not change, regardless of how far up the ladder he made it in his clique.

"It's a great day for some shooting practice. It's a pleasure to drive when it's like this outside, I never understood why you don't drive more yourself," he said.

"I don't know, I don't really feel like going places. It's good to have a car, but I didn't use it in a long while."

"That's the problem with you, you just stay home, go to the store, go back home and that's it. If it wasn't for me, you might not even know we have all this nature surrounding us."

"If it wasn't for you, I'd probably think the

world is flat," I countered.

"No, seriously. I'm guessing you haven't been to this place yet, where we're heading now."

"Where is that?"

"Once you cross the bridge, you go opposite where we went last time, to the valley. It's pretty close to the river; behind the old quarry, there's a place like a plateau or something. It's not too far, but it's kind of hidden; it's a perfect spot to practice shooting, I used to go there every weekend."

"Until you became the sharpshooter that you are today," I heckled.

"Exactly."

"As if I don't know where that is. I had my first kiss close to that place."

"Maybe you lost your virginity at that quarry too, I imagine that's why you haven't left the house in the last ten years," he taunted me again.

"Which would still be better than how you lost yours."

"I handed it to you on a plate, my bad."

Bone had lost his virginity in unusual circumstances during a cabin trip after being dared by his friends to make the big move on his girlfriend in one of the hammocks there as if the first time doing it doesn't feel strange enough.

Something I liked about Bone was how we went toe to toe when it came to banter, and knew the right time when to stop, right before pushing one another over the edge. Every now and again, people mistook us for siblings, not entirely due to our synergy, but also thanks to our physical aspect.

Without realizing it, we reached the quarry. Going around it, Bone parked the car so that no one could see it there unless they bypassed the curtain of trees and the quarry itself.

"Look at 'em shine," he said pulling out two guns from under the driver's seat. Indeed, they were black and must have been recently cleaned, as the sunlight glanced off their surface.

"I haven't seen a gun before. It feels like we're in America or something."

"You'd be surprised how many people have firearms in this town. And that's only the people I know," Bone emphasized.

He handed me a gun, putting the other under his belt. Then he lit a cigarette and got out.

"Is it possible that you blow your balls off that way?"

"If you cock the gun, maybe. See?" he took out the weapon, pointed it at me, and pressed the trigger. Instinctively, I flinched, although I was aware he wouldn't shoot me.

"Let's focus on the mannequins, alright?" I asked him.

"Sure thing. Come on, help me carry them."

In the trunk were the two mannequins, designed to resemble an ectomorph male torso, with the neck and head included. They could hardly be described, apart from how plain and uninspiring they were, and that they were made out of plastic. They were also missing their arms, with their heads and faces being crudely shaped. Bone picked one up and headed away from the car. I did so as well.

"This has got to be one of my weirder Tuesday noons so far," I admitted.

"I'm sure you've had worse. Here, this will do," Bone said placing his mannequin on a log, propped up against a branch. "You can leave the other one, for now, let's mow down this one first."

We walked away. At about fifteen meters, Bone put a stick down as a marker.

"This is the closest you can shoot from. Otherwise, it ain't practice anymore, just a waste of bullets."

"I thought you said it'd be just for fun, but I should've thought you meant your fun."

He didn't say anything; instead, he raised the gun, took aim, and missed his shot.

"Hell, I must have lost it a bit. Actually, I just don't wanna make you feel bad."

"Much appreciated. I bet you missed on purpose, possibly to get me into a shooting contest or something."

"Now that doesn't sound too bad. Care to make it interesting?"

I didn't answer him; instead, I raised the

weapon, focused as much as I could, took aim, and pressed the trigger, my first time firing a gun. Neither of us could figure out where the bullet went, but it surely missed the target.

"Wow," Bone said, "maybe it's a bit early for a contest. Somewhere in these woods, a squirrel is missing its nuts right now."

"If you ever forget to block the gun before putting it in your pants, I'll remind you about this."

A flock of birds ascended from the trees and flew in our direction, above the quarry and away from our shooting stand. Bone pointed his piece at the birds.

"What do I get if I bring one down?"

"Two bullets in the head and five in the chest. You're closer than the mannequin, so I wouldn't risk it if I were you."

"Relax, I'm kidding. How about this; if I get a body shot, I score a point. A headshot is three points. You get double for your shots. The winner gets twenty bucks and the last to three has to do a hundred pushups."

"Easy on the numbers, man. Give me some warm-up shots first, then I'll consider it. How expensive are these bullets, by the way?"

"They're free because I know a guy. Or some guys...Look, here it is," he said taking out a plastic bag full of ammo, "I don't have extra mags, but we can take these out and load them by hand."

"OK."

I took a few shots and missed all of them. Not that I'd ever thought about firing guns, although I wouldn't have guessed aiming could be so difficult. Or maybe I was simply bad at it. Bone took off his jacket in the meantime and sat on it to smoke. While holding a firearm did have an effect on me, quite similar to cocaine in a way, I thought, in terms of boosting the ego, it definitely didn't have enough to keep mc cngaged for long. Until then, focused on the target, the gun, and the competition with Bone, I'd blocked out all else surrounding me. Which made no sense, since I wouldn't have come there in the first place on a rainy day. Thus, I took a moment to breathe the clear, fresh air, to enjoy the sun's caress on my skin, the various sounds of nature, and, of course, the beautiful motley of colors in front of me. The next shot I took hit the mannequin, chipping its left shoulder.

"Shall we start the count?" Bone asked.

"Yeah, why not."

There was also an odd sensation of bonding in trusting an armed person next to you, especially since Bone didn't pay attention to me, apart from when he heard the plastic shattering, as he otherwise checked his phone or simply scanned the area rather than keep an eye on me. Being so calm around an armed person constituted a great deal of strength and self-confidence, besides the obvious friendship.

I fired eight or ten further shots. I asked Bone how many bullets were in the magazine. About twenty, he answered. I told him I wasn't going to shoot that much, opting rather for a walk instead.

"I see. How about the first to seven shots on target wins twenty bucks and that's that?"

"You're really keen on them gains, aren't you?"

"Well, I basically taught you how to shoot, there should something in it for me too at least."

"I see. The floor is yours, Rambo."

Rambo took ten shots to reach his goal. Before my turn came, I asked about mounting the other mannequin, as the first one nearly disintegrated under our shots.

It didn't make much sense since the plastic at the back remained intact. The front - so the belly, chest, and throat of the mannequin were shredded. A large hole also stretched from the forehead across to the left cheek of our target. I stepped up but preventing us from continuing the destruction, Bone's phone rang.

"What's good? What, already? You need me? We gotta clean up too, or...? Oh, alright. Yeah, I got you covered," he said glancing at my weapon. "Nah, it's fine, I'm ready to bounce. OK, see ya in a bit."

"Now?" I asked.

"We can finish this first, it's not too urgent."

I fired the gun seven times and managed to hit the target twice. After that, I handed the weapon back to its owner, along with the cash.

"Easiest cash I ever made," he smirked.

"Good for you. I hope you're not leaving those behind," I pointed at the mannequins.

"I guess we can take them with us. You can actually keep the good one, who knows when it could come in handy. Or when I get the chance to snatch some more."

"Me? Why do I have to keep it?"

"I'll drop you off, but then I gotta be somewhere. I'm not bringing that thing with me."

We headed towards the massacred piece of plastic. Behind it, the vegetation and its inhabitants lay silent, as if gauging our next move, us being the equivalent of the loud obnoxious intruders. Bone grabbed the mannequin on the ground, whereas I tried to clean up as many of the blown-off pieces as possible before heading back to the car.

Glancing back at our practice spot, grey clouds slowly approached from the distance, threatening to blot the sun once again. The sunny day was, in fact, a rare occurrence during that time of year, being more of a gift than a sign of promise for the coming days. The log, standing against the quiet, unmoving trees behind it, evoked the image of a gallows, with the sober crowd having witnessed the execution. A cold shiver ran through me; I didn't want to fire a gun again. For a second, my perception of Bone changed, turning him from a friend into a distant, unrelated character.

Opposite to the cruise on the way here, now we were rushing to make it back quickly so Bone could meet his crew in time. He rarely exhibited signs of stress, although I was certain he didn't think he afforded to be as casual as he normally came across. His smile faded; an uncharacteristically serious expression took its place.

Snapping me out of an unpleasant contemplation, my phone rang. It was Richie, my problematic friend. He often called at a bad time, and the minutes spent talking to him were also bad.

"Hey, what's up?" I said, trying not to sound too irritated.

"I remember you asked me to be blunt from now on, so can you lend me forty bucks? I've got a great tip on the games this week and don't want to lose it."

"You know I don't like this. If you needed food or something, no problem, but I don't agree with giving you money to piss it away on betting."

"I'm aware, but I promise I'll give it back after it's done. I'm telling you, Chris, these games are a lock. I'd ask my mom for the money, though I wanted to ask you first. Why don't you come by for a beer later?"

"I don't feel like drinking today."

"Right...Jane and Sophia are coming in a couple of weeks, by the way, I thought it'd be nice to have some cash so I can take them out or something."

Hearing that riled me greatly. Jane was his ex-wife and Sophia their daughter. Jane divorced him after he became an alcoholic, quit his job, and started wasting money on bets and booze. We'd both courted Jane in high school, although she chose him over me. Richie knew I still had a soft spot for her, and occasionally hinted at it to his benefit, as he did now. While not being with Jane obviously hurt me, I didn't hold any grudges against her; not even against Richie at first, only after he lost control of himself. It also hurt when they had Sophia; I knew that would irreversibly shatter all my chances of being with Jane, and that I'd probably never experience that happiness in my life. Then, years later, the day Jane took Sophia and left the house because of Richie's behavior, I had such a clear and distinct sensation that I would kill him one day. Anyhow, I didn't hold on to that thought. Also, I didn't hate Richie, nor did I need to; I simply disregarded him.

"So what do you say?" he continued.

"I'll think about it," I said and hung up.

"Acid tongue." Bone likely weighed whether or not to make that remark, gauging my disposition first.

"Perfectly justifiable in this case. Rich stepped on my nerves again."

"Oh."

"I remember how my mom used to get annoyed at drunk people. The older I get, the more I follow in her footsteps."

"Interesting that you're saying that, the same happens with me and my pops. We have identical tastes in cars and women. It must be genetic or something."

We continued the trip back in silence. Not long after, we reached my flat. I shook Bone's hand and pressed the door handle to leave when he reminded me to take the mannequin upstairs.

"You sure you can't just leave it in the trunk?" I tried to avoid bringing that piece of trash into my apartment. What would happen next was that I would ask Bone repeatedly how much longer I had to keep it, to which he would inevitably answer that he'd pick it up soon. Then, right as I'd throw it away, he'd ask me about the mannequin.

"Yes, no doubt about it. Besides, Bella wouldn't like it if I brought it home. Sorry, buddy."

Thus, I conformed and took it with me. Turning around to wave, Bone had already left in a hurry. Impressive how he managed to joke around and stay easygoing, given the demands of his job. Guys like him rarely have a decent life expectancy, unfortunately; I had to enjoy him while he was still around.

Climbing up with that chunk of plastic in my arms, which for some reason felt heavier than before, I recalled having to visit Mrs. Trent to check up on her sickness. She generally took care of herself since she lived alone, with her husband having passed away and her daughter working abroad. However, Mrs. Trent was suffering from a bout of flu and previously seemed weak and tired, so I wanted to take care of her. Not as if she asked me or anything, just that I'd feel bad if I didn't.

First, I dropped off the mannequin at mine. Thinking of grabbing a bite before getting some groceries for my neighbor, I walked in absent-mindedly with my shoes on. I opened the storage room and made space for the mannequin among the boxes, pots, and compost bags then set it down between them. However, as a weak shard of light coming through the half-open door highlighted the mannequin, it raised an odd awareness of sharing the room with it, a togetherness unmediated by anyone else's presence. In the penumbra of that confined space, the obscure light fell right on the inexpressive piece of plastic I'd brought into my house, now eerily glaring at me in its bleak, icy silence. Unnerved, I skipped food and headed straight to the store, as if to escape that suffocating, invasive presence, locking the storage room behind me.

The store had a steady flow of customers throughout most of the week, apart from the spikes on Saturday morning and evening. We, the staff, saw the same faces again and again, who, in part, saw the same three people again and again, which gave the store an air of familiarity and permanence, turning it into a cornerstone in our community.

Inside I found George, busy typing at the cash register, with a customer in front of him and another waiting in line. He acknowledged my presence with a nod. I waved in reply, then went straight to the backroom. Kim had done a good job, as always, with everything perfectly organized and ready to be taken out to restock the empty shelves. The back room was rather tiny, so I figured I needed a woman's spatial awareness for that job. Storing all those boxes and keeping the room clean on top of that resembled a messy game of Tetris, which Kim effortlessly bossed.

Before moving on to fill the cold shelves with beers and soda, plus a couple of bean cans on the neighboring shelf, I checked the notebook in the cupboard by the door. The previous day's orders were already noted down; Kim seldom backlogged herself. One aspect I took care of by myself was the accountancy; it made no sense to dent my profit by hiring someone since I had so much spare time. Plus, the number crunching came in good on occasion, keeping me busy and my mind sharp.

The front of the store had cleared up in the meanwhile. George came from behind the counter to shake my hand.

"Had a rough one last night," he said stretching his back.

"Same here a few nights ago actually. Nothing bad though, I hope?"

"No, no, I went to a friend's birthday and couldn't leave early. I didn't want to, either, we were having a lot of fun, but I just kept thinking how I'd regret it in the morning," he snickered. "What about you?"

"Had to take care of some stuff, move around a bunch of furniture, you know. A few years ago it would've been fine, but now I feel like I'm digging my own grave whenever I work late," I made an innuendo to myself.

"Yeah, I can't drink like I used to either. These hangovers keep getting worse every time, I swear. Mind if take a cigarette break?"

"Not at all, go for it."

"Alright. I'mma make some coffee, you want some?" George said heading to the back, where we kept the machine.

"Sure, thanks."

Watching out for customers, I began shopping for Mrs. Trent. When I asked what to bring her, once I finally convinced her to let me help out, she said whatever, preferably some older products in the store, so they wouldn't end up going to waste. Obviously, I picked out what I knew came in good for sickness. First, ginger and lemons for tea, hoping she had honey at home. Then some oranges, apples, bananas, garlic, two cans of broth (we didn't have whole chickens), and vegetables for soup. Halfway through my list, George brought me the coffee. I stopped him on his way:

"Did you notice who keeps ripping the bananas open? They never last longer than a few days," I spoke. The way bananas came in bunches, bound together by that woody part, someone repeatedly ripped them in such a way that all the peels in the bunch would split open, revealing the flesh of the fruit, which naturally degraded sooner than normal.

"Can't say that I have, but I did notice the bananas were messed up. I'll keep an eye out from now on."

One customer walked in. I waited for a second to see if George followed him inside. He did. I continued picking up provisions for Mrs. Trent until my phone rang again. I cringed for a second, thinking it was Richie. Luckily, it was Jane.

"Jane, hi! How are you guys doing? I missed

your voice."

"Hey Chris, I missed you too, it's been a while. We're fine, Sophia is right here with me. Say hi to Chris, Soph."

"HIIII CHRIS!" she shouted, unleashing her excitement.

Hearing them both instantly restored my good mood. I cared deeply about them. In a way, they were my family too.

"Hey, sweetic. I heard we're going to see each other soon," I said previous to hearing her giggling in the background.

"So we're planning," Jane said. "We'll try to book a flight at the beginning of next month sometime, I can't wait to see everyone again. How've you been, is everything alright?"

"Same old, same old, things rarely change around here. Is anyone picking you up from the airport, by the way? Let me know if you need a ride."

"Don't worry about it, it's all taken care of. However, since you mentioned it, we might drop by Soph's grandparents for a day or so, could I borrow your car maybe? Approximately around the 11th or 12th."

"Absolutely, you know you always can."

Rich's parents lived relatively close, although in a somewhat remote area. They loved Sophia and Sophia loved them, therefore Jane didn't stand between them and took her daughter to visit every time they came home. Rich's relationship with his parents had been naturally strained in the previous years, so it fell on Jane to preserve the connection with that side of the family, for Sophia's sake.

"Thanks a lot, I owe you one. By the way, since we missed your birthday, we got you something, Soph came up with the idea. Anyway, talking on the phone has never been my strong point, I know you don't like it either, so...I'm really looking forward to catching up with you, Chris. We'll see each other soon."

"Me too. Let me know when you guys land. Safe travels, girls. Bye Sophia," I said, sensing how she anticipated her moment.

"BYEEE CHRIS!" she yelled.

I left the store with a heavy shopping bag in my hand, whose contents were strategically selected to sustain a perfect three-day diet meant to heal Mrs. Trent completely. Entering the building, I noticed any trace of the roach infestation had vanished, there were no tiny black dots whatsoever to be seen. Loud fragments of music in the hallway gave away that the couple on the first floor was home. On the other hand, upstairs, Mrs. Trent listened to classical music. Often when I visited, I found her playing that. She saw the large bag in my hand and seemed ashamed.

"Why are you doing this, why are you wasting your weekend on me? You're young, there are many other things you could be doing instead," she said, rushing to change the music.

"Leave it, it's very nice. I had to go by the store anyway. Wouldn't you do the same for me?"

"Of course, but I never get the chance. Thank you so much, though I can't help but feel old when you're taking care of me, and we're not even related. I don't want you to think of me that way."

"You're the only one thinking that way, and I'm sure you know it."

"You're too kind..."

I went and sat on the armchair opposite the couch. In the meantime, Mrs. Trent drew the curtains and opened the windows to let fresh air into the room. Our apartments were similar in size and had been designed the same way, though Mrs. Trent's was cozier and much more welcoming, understandably. Comfort blended with good taste and modesty, which reflected in everything in that apartment, from the furniture to the accessories, the few paintings on the walls, and the way my neighbor dressed – wearing plainly colored but quality clothes. Mrs. Trent lived her life with much dignity, although it must've been difficult to age alone and have only a few people to talk to.

"Oh, I hope you're not going to get sick too from staying here, I'd be mad at myself. No, actually, I'd be mad at you!" she joked, half frowning half smiling at me at the same time.

"I'll have to take my chances on this one. By the way, we don't have chickens at the store, so I hope you can make do with just broth."

"Don't be silly, you've already done too much. I'll work wonders with what you brought."

She continued swooshing around, putting things in their place and making the room nice and suitable for receiving guests. Even though I lived next door, she always did that. I knew it made no sense to try to stop her, especially since it made her feel better.

"It's good you came, or I might have wasted the whole day slacking off," she said.

"I can't stay long Mrs. T, maybe you can do this later and sit down with me for a bit?"

"Oh, yes, of course," she said evidently put off in her agitation. "You've got to have a cup of tea, at least, I'll go boil some water."

"Could I have a coffee instead? I'm not big on..."

"Yes, yes, I forgot, you don't like tea," she interrupted me in her rush. "I'll be with you in a moment."

"You could make yourself some ginger tea, by the way," I said getting up to take the ginger and lemons out of the bag. "Do you have honey?"

Although she said she never got the chance to take care of me, it wasn't true. Mrs. Trent often brought over soups, stews, cakes, and generally any food she made that could be shared. She had a motherly concern for me, especially for what I ate. At first, I refused politely, but I realized she needed someone to care for, and I happened to fill that gap perfectly. I didn't mind, since she was an excellent cook. Whenever my neighbor made more than one portion, we ate it together, usually at her place, alleviating her loneliness as well as mine.

"Do you mind if I close the window?" Mrs. Trent asked. "You couldn't tell we're in November right now, if not for that cold gust outside. The trees are only starting to shed," she spoke looking outside.

Nature lasted longer that year, as it did the previous year compared to the one before. While my own psychological time seemed to have frozen at some point in my early adulthood, the universal time slowly followed suit. Soon, the world will reach a place, above and outside of its history, when all things and people become stationary, suspended in our being, and nothing new will come to be, no new people will be born; the world will be saturated with existence, so everything will crystalize in a perfect state of universal consciousness, from which we'll then gradually and peacefully fade away.

The tips of the branches began to yellow and grow tired, bearing the occasional rough showers during the days combined with the cold of the nights, draining the life out of the least protected, more outward leaves. This is why Mrs. Trent's apartment, with its light brown furniture, beige carpets and walls, and autumnal paintings fully came to life during the fall season.

"I wish you could see our home in France when my husband still lived," she began telling me. "I've already shown you some photos, but it's not the same when you see it in person. We lived in Brive, a diamond of a village. We had evergreens in our garden, and the seasons changed so subtly and gently. I'm glad my daughter chose France over other places, I'm really happy for her. The one thing I can't understand is why on earth she decided to live in Paris when there are so many wonderful areas in that country where you don't feel smothered when you leave the house," she laughed.

"She can always move somewhere else once she's had enough there," I said.

Mrs. Trent smiled in agreement. Whenever she mentioned her daughter, more so than her husband even, loneliness emanated from her like an aura, stirring in me a bittersweet melancholy. Having recovered from the earlier incident with the mannequin, I remembered not eating since breakfast, as the night subtly encroached on us while chatting. Eventually, we wished each other a good night, not before establishing to meet again the following noon.

Finally at home, capping off another ordinary weekday, I could take care of something I'd been looking forward to since waking up, which was to water my peach seedlings. The sun would soon no longer shine generously over them, so my plants were about to leave behind their first vegetative period and embrace the dark, cold months of dormancy ahead of them. I fed them the last quarter of the one-liter bottle I'd mixed water and fertilizer in, as the heavy feeding would be resumed again around March or April. Until then, they had to do solely with plain water.

Alas, one of my seedlings showed some slightly worrying signs, since the younger leaves turned pale in the areas between the dark, central veins. This indicated an iron deficiency, be it from a lack of iron in the soil, or the soil not being acidic enough for the plant to be able to absorb the nutrients. Which was weird, since I'd used the same soil for all my four plants, and fed them exactly the same substances. I hoped they could get through the coming months unscathed, although from the second I emptied the bottle on the afflicted seedling, until nestling in my bed, protected from the screeching wind and the cold draughts seeping through underneath the old windows, a certain emptiness took over me, leaving me vulnerable in the face of the suddenly and inexplicably ominous future.

Chapter III

The next morning Bone called me down for a quick ride. I didn't ask why, since he probably couldn't say on the phone. Out under the grey clouds and the cold wind, the Audi was already there.

"Slept well?" Bone asked, starting the car.

"Don't remember. You?"

"I wanted to hand you the gift," he said taking out an envelope from the dashboard. "Extra spicy, as promised."

I took it, not without some disgust that I hadn't previously felt. I could lend some of the money straight to Ritchie however, so it was alright. I put the envelope under my belt but Bone kept driving around.

"Thanks. I'm guessing there's more you wanted to tell me though."

"Yeah," he answered. "I'm paying you now because I'll be a little busy for a while. There've been some rumors going on recently and I don't like what I'm hearing, so maybe I'll be asked to do something about it."

"What happened?"

"Nothing certain yet, but I wanted to see if you could help me out in a week or two, if necessary."

"Well yeah, in theory, but I can't give you my word until you fill me in."

"Of course. I'm just giving you a heads up, that's all."

We did a lap of the town center and then he drove me back. Seeing Bone lighting a cigarette with unusual agitation gave me a bad feeling in my gut. Despite what he told me, maybe the shooting practice had a purpose after all. The sight of the mannequin flashed in my head, rigidly waiting for its execution. Regardless of our roles, it still gave the impression that I was the one unsafe, and only the cold outside made me shake off that perception.

Back in my building, a fine scent imbued the air. Knocking on Mrs. Trent's door, she greeted me with a wide smile. Her outfit signaled she had recently returned home, or that she planned to leave soon. The same fragrance as that from the hallway emanated from her knitted long scarf.

"Hello, Chris. I just went and bought some of those biscuits you like, to have with your coffee. I wanted to ask you to join me for a walk soon, although those clouds may have plans on their own."

"Yes, it's pretty chilly outside, better to stay in for now."

Bending to untie my shoes, the envelope from Bone slipped away from my belt, with a couple of bills flying out of it. Mrs. Trent turned around and saw them, then looked at me. I instantly dodged her eyes, picking up the envelope and sliding it back in place.

"Would you like cream with your coffee?" she asked almost immediately.

"Yes please."

I sat down on an armchair, studying the details of the painting in front of me. Two miniature poorly dressed figures, presumably peasants, were portrayed strolling down a road through a myriad of faded nuances of yellow, orange, and light brown. The figures were trudging sluggishly, suggesting that they were returning from the field following a hard day's work. Under a bland sky, the mud trail stretched from the bottom-right up to the middle-left section of the painting, growing narrow and creating the illusion of distance, as well as the vanishing point of the painting. The two subdued, disheveled figures steered towards it. There were many ways to interpret the painting, other than the simple pleasure of just enjoying the beautiful colors and the serene subject matter; however, they were all centered around an inescapable desolation.

First, my neighbor put the bowl of biscuits on the wooden table between us followed by the two cups, mine with coffee, hers with tea.

"How's the illness coming along? Are you feeling better than yesterday?" I asked prior to sipping on my drink.

"I am, thanks to the ginger, it helped with my sore throat. What have you been up to this morning?"

"I...just went for a ride with a friend, tried to take advantage before it gets too cold," I answered cautiously.

"That's nice, I'm glad you did."

"Recently we went over the bridge and stopped somewhere along the river for a little while. Very pretty area."

"You can go as often as you want. You own a car, right?" she asked.

"Sure, though I'm usually not in the mood to go for rides randomly by myself."

I instantly wished I hadn't said that, since I could have invited her to join me anytime, yet never did.

"You know," she continued, "this might come out of the blue, but I worry about you sometimes."

"How come?"

"Well, again, I hope you don't mind my saying, as this is coming from a friend and someone who could be your mother altogether, age-wise," she said affectionately. "There's something uncommonly...steady about you, given your age, your preoccupations, your choice of friends, and here I'm referring to myself."

"I purely enjoy my quiet moments, that's all. No need to be concerned, really Mrs. T."

"No, that's not all; also your relationship status – and this is not my business at all – but I'm assuming you're single as well and from what I can gather you spend most of your time either at home, at the store or having coffee with me. While I very much enjoy your company, I can't help but think you should be doing other things at this stage in your life."

Holding the teacup in her hand, her frail aspect, conferred by old age and the clearly outlined veins running along her tainted skin, visibly worried about upsetting me, Mrs. T waited for me to say or do something before she drank. Her concern was innocent and sincere; while she'd never addressed it as seriously as she did now, I'd braced myself for that question. Regardless, I didn't have much to say on the matter, since I truly had nothing to hide.

"I imagine it can seem a bit suspicious, although there's nothing to say about it. I enjoy spending time by myself for the most part, other than seeing you or that friend of mine I told you about. I rarely get bored when I'm alone, in fact."

"Alright," she said, bordering between appeasement and doubt. "I'm not in your shoes, we lived completely different lives so I can't tell you what to do and what not to do. But I hope you won't get stuck, feel lonely, or even worse, end up losing yourself, God forbid."

I sensed she made a reference to the envelope with the last remark. My brief life story remained a mystery for Mrs. Trent, which went both ways because we didn't bother with unearthing each other's past. She did offer me glimpses of her youth and time in France with her husband, although few and far between, perhaps unlike many people her age. Again, dignity constituted a great part of her overall character, which ensured our relationship didn't extend beyond the moments we spent together in our daily life; we had a healthy respect, combined with disinterest in one another's private history.

On the other hand, an envelope full of money hidden under my belt failed to align with the image she'd created of me, however vague it might have been.

"So far I've been good this way," I spoke. "It feels as if I'm still winding down after something happened, yet I can't put my finger on what exactly."

"I understand. I'm doing the same, to be

honest. As much as I enjoyed teaching, for example, I probably wouldn't do it again."

"Why is that?"

"That passion burned out in me. One year after reaching retirement age, I decided to quit. It happened quite organically. You always realize when the right moment comes to stop doing something. The harder part is to accept it, sometimes."

"But you still read books."

"Definitely, the reading is here to stay."

She poured herself more tea from the kettle. Meanwhile, I'd finished the coffee, without touching the biscuits.

"You own a car if I'm not mistaken, right?" she asked suddenly. It was the first time she repeated herself, something which I noticed would happen increasingly in the future. I said nothing about it.

"Yes, why?"

"I thought of buying a tree for Christmas this year, in case my daughter comes to visit. One of those artificial ones, of course. Could you help me bring it home?"

"Gladly, let me know when and we'll take care of it."

Later, when Mrs. Trent's washing machine beeped, I took the chance to leave, not without asking if she needed any help with the laundry, expecting her to politely refuse, which she did. On my way to Ritchie, I quickly dropped by mine to change my jacket for a thicker one, as the wind outside now howled and shrieked menacingly, despite the shining sun.

Richie lived in a small old house his parent invested in and passed on to him once he started his family. Needless to say, he didn't take care of it; the uncut grass was riddled with twigs and one large branch had fallen off one of the chestnut trees in the yard. Richie had long sold his car, along with the garage on the other side of the street to fund his listless celibacy. I understood not wanting to be tied down to a nine-to-five for five days a week, therefore I didn't judge him for not working; what I condemned him for was not looking after what could have been one of the most beautiful properties in town, a place where any regular working person wouldn't mind spending their retirement years. I took the key, hanging from the inside of the fence on the opposite corner from where the door was, removed the crowbar enforcing the lock, and knocked on Richie's door. After a good minute, he opened.

"Chris, thanks for coming man, I feared the weather might have put you off. I'm glad it didn't."

"What's up," I said. When a man becomes so

isolated and tries his best to cut off every tie with the outside world, there are only so many things you can talk with him about.

"Come on, I'll show you what's up." The house remained as Jane organized it, though much less clean compared to when she lived there. We sat on the couch and he began showing me his betting history, followed by some statistics on the games that were about to take place that night. Richie was so engaged in his analysis, talking as if he was alone in the house; listening to him, I witnessed what happened when people end up spending too much time with their thoughts. He snapped out of it to ask me abruptly:

"Do you want a beer? I forgot to offer you one. Let me get the ashtray too." Then he got up to bring two beers and a pack of cigarettes. He took one out before offering me one as well.

"Sure," I accepted. "How much do you want to bet?"

"A hundred, all of it on these three matches. The odds aren't that great, but that's because it's a safe bet. We can split the gains afterwards. I thought of taking a break and finding a job online or something, you know, to try and get back in the game."

"Aha, it'd be a good move," I said skeptically.

"No, really. I only need a bit of cash while

looking for a job. Plus, I wanted to get Sophia something too; I didn't buy her anything in a long while..."

"What if you lose the bet?"

He continued staring at the laptop, ignoring my question. Clearly, he didn't want to think about it. I'd given him money previously to take out Sophia and treat her to something, acting like an actual father, but I told him I wouldn't do it again.

I sipped on my beer and wandered through the room, stopping in front of the window to look at the two chestnuts guarding the house. Then I turned around and looked at Richie, lost in thought over the odds, with his dark, messy hair, short shave, and grey tracksuit. One can't afford to passively allow time to fly over, but try to actively advance through it, or at least tag along. The consequences of failing to do so can be truly alienating.

"Alrighty, that's that then. I'll run quickly over to the agency before it closes, then we can have some beers and watch the games. You can sleep here if you want, there's going to be a storm tonight."

"Don't worry, I didn't plan to stay long, I've got some stuff to do," I said placing a bill on the table. For some reason, I parted more easily with the money from Bone than with what I earned from the store.

"Oh, as you wish," he said with a dejected look, probably realizing his break from loneliness had come to an end. "Thanks, Chris, I'll let you know about the bet," Rich said in a guilty tone, standing up to shake my hand.

I fought the fierce wind on my way home. Indeed, a great storm washed over our town that night. The chestnuts in front of Richie's house were being swept brutally when I left, reminding me of a painting of trees being ripped apart and uprooted by a biblical storm.

Seeing my flat building filled me with a snuggly sensation; natural events put us back in touch with the primordial importance of shelters and our need for safety, which is one of the reasons I loved storms. The other critters enjoyed it less; a single cockroach, again, crawling slowly, decrepitly on the hallway floor. It had probably been poisoned. Many of them lived in the attic, feeding on pigeon droppings, as well as on each other's carcasses, presumably. Whenever it rained, they fell to death out of the attic, making for a repulsive picture the following day.

I finally found myself back in my apartment, having seen another day through. Stumbling into the pitch-black living room, I easily located the lamp in the corner of the room and turned it on. I'd made the walk to the lamp in the dark so many times, I could do it in any circumstances. An intimate, honey-like light animated the room, recreating that safe ambiance I craved at the end of every day. A dimly lit room, in contrast to the black all-encompassing night outside, and a warm meal alleviated all my problems.

It took me a split second to decide what to make for dinner: the ultimate feel-good meal for me, pasta. I took out the large pot, a sieve, and frying pan from the cupboard by my knees, filled up the pot with water, and sat it on the stove. Opening the fridge, it appeared dinner would be frugal that night, for the shelves were almost empty. I got so caught up with Bone, Rich, and Mrs. Trent that I forgot to take care of my own needs again. Fortunately, the store waited at my disposal right across the street. However, I still had some onions, cheddar cheese, and half a bag of frozen green peas. I'd made that recipe before; therefore, after turning on the speakers to play ambient music, I dripped some olive oil into the pan and began dicing one large onion. The green peas lay next to the cutting board, defrosting in the stainless-steel bowl, in which I'd also pour the dish once cooked. Soon, I mixed the peas with the onion in the pan and added some pasta water, all while stirring into the pot so the pasta wouldn't stick. Then I drained the pasta and dropped it into the pan as well, cooking the ingredients together, sprinkling salt and pepper, and grating a large amount of cheese. I also added a piece of butter to make the dish creamier.

For the next hour, I ate, listened to music, and did the dishes, so as to not wake up to a full sink the following morning. Slowly my body became languid, slipping into that sweet lethargy preceding sleep, but a thought popped up in my mind which could not bear postponement; with one last effort for the day, I went to read the label of the fertilizer used on the peach trees, hoping I had the special one with added iron, not another type.

I opened the storage room and the first thing to jump at me was the sight of the mannequin, surrounded by the same unsettling energy. I had to turn the light there to ease my nerves. However, I decided not to allow it to spoil my night; thus, I picked up the fertilizer and came out quickly, locking the door behind me. Indeed, I had the special fertilizer; my peach seedlings should turn out fine.

I wanted to take another look at my beautiful, healthy plants before hitting the sack. To my dismay, I saw one of the peaches covered by a plague of tiny white bugs, swarming up and down its stem and along the leaves. Their apparition made no sense, I couldn't think of any place they could have come from, especially in such great numbers and as swiftly as they did. Up and down, up and down, they streamed without relent, feeding on the leaf and root tissue, burying my plant alive, plunging it into illness and killing it, then certain to spread on to the others too. Their swarm was a sickening display. Then, all of a sudden, a terrible flush hit me: my knees buckled and my vision turned black, with the entire room spinning around me as I lost my consciousness and passed out on the floor.

Chapter IV

Early in the morning, I went in a hurry to buy pesticide. To be fair, I stayed idle for a few minutes until Kim had enough time to open, to avoid running into her on my way out of the building. Not that I minded her; in fact, I admired Kim for her character and pleasant way of being, though some mornings simply required you to avoid others.

One additional reason besides my haste was the bruise on the side of my head. I preferred not having to explain it to anyone. I'd also hurt my hip, where my skin turned yellow with a purple blot in the middle. Thankfully, I collapsed next to the plants and not on them.

At around 9 o'clock I had already come back. I also used my car at last, though not in the most agreeable of circumstances. I quickly diluted the solution and sprayed it on all the plants. The label specified it could take up to an hour to kill the insects. As long as it got the job done, it should be alright.

Going to put the bottle in the storage out of habit, along with any new object, so to preserve the order in the house, the door remained closed when I pressed the knob. The reason for that came to mind at once, but instead of the terror from the previous day, now I was mad at the mannequin, blaming it for my accident. Inevitably, I thought of Richie. It happened whenever my disposition worsened. He owed me money, so I'd better go pick it up before he thought too much about betting it and gave in to temptation.

It was still fairly early. If I went by his place then, there would still be time left to go to the store later and raise my spirits. Another custom passed on by my mom, or lesson rather, taught me how to calm down by redirecting my negative energy towards something productive, namely cleaning. She'd been a stickler when it came to cleanliness for two reasons: such had her mother, my grandmother, raised her, punishing her if the house didn't sparkle by when she returned from work. The punishment consisted of slapping, berating, or throwing things at her, whatever my grandmother had at hand. Once, the handiest object happened to be a pot of boiling water. My grandmother never hesitated when applying her punishment, perhaps because she'd also been brought up like that. My mother bore the reddish mark on her leg for her entire life.

Secondly, the more fortunate reason behind her compulsion to clean, was her learning to transform duties into pleasant activities. My mother had been a smart woman, and she could have surely had a better life if not for the severely limiting circumstances.

I planned to make it to the store right ahead of the closing hour. That way, I could calm down after meeting Richie, as well as help Kim and spare her from having to refill the shelves or mop the floor.

Stretching upwards to the sky, along my way to Richie's house, the various types of trees scattered throughout the town. I couldn't identify all of them off the top of my head, but I knew the ones with dark purple leaves were Japanese cherry trees. In the spring they bloomed into a beautiful pink adorned with white flowers, whose short-lived petals later coated the ground. Younger people didn't seem to pay much attention to them, except for the photos they took from time to time. Older people and children, on the other hand, rejoiced in the spectacle of nature. We had other trees too around the Japanese cherries; some turned yellow, orange, or burgundy, and a few stayed green right until full-fledged winter. The majority of colors blended together in my town during the cold season, not least because they were all somewhat bland; the heavy dust ensured the recent, sharper colors quickly became dull.

The ashy sky above completed the

chromatic composition for the day. The wind had ceased, so the cold made way for a toothless chill. I arrived at Richie's house, forever guarded by the two stern chestnuts. I wriggled my hand through the fence bars, patting around for the key. I hated how in the summer there were always cobwebs in that corner, however, there were no surprises this time. Walking on the pathway, I paid attention not to step on any snails. No snail had been crushed around, meaning that my friend hadn't left the house recently.

At the end of my usual minute of waiting, Rich answered.

"Are you from the IRS?" he said from behind the door.

"Yes, unfortunately, we've come to seize this property. Would you kindly let me in, sir?"

"Out of necessity, I will. Would a beer help pave the way for an amicable discussion instead?" he proposed on his way to the fridge.

"Perhaps."

I went and sat down on the couch. The setting kept its consistently orderly appearance, yet dirty under a closer examination. Rich came with the beers and ashtray, freshly emptied.

"What did you make?" I asked.

"On that ticket? About five hundred. But I went the next day and put it all on a new bet. In total, your hundred generated a fifteen hundred profit margin," he said proudly. The first half of the sentence he uttered with pride, then changed his tone to a cautious one, suddenly aware that I was entitled to some of the earnings.

"Nice."

"Yeah."

I decided to tease him a bit and let him wait to find out how much of it I wanted.

"Got an opener?" I asked about the beer.

"Yeah, sure. How much should I give you?"

"What do you mean?"

"The money, how much do you want?"

"It's up to me to choose, you mean?"

It was mean of me, but I continued playing.

"Yeah, yeah."

"Oh, well then...I remember you mentioned something about splitting it half and half?"

"Uhm, did I?"

"Didn't you? Maybe I'm wrong, I don't remember."

"I mean, we could, but you didn't know about the second bet," he spoke, fidgeting and ripping up the label on the bottle.

"True, though wouldn't that entitle me to more?"

"How is that?"

"Well, you went behind my back and placed another bet. If you lost, you couldn't afford to pay me back for the initial bet. Shouldn't there be a policy regarding that situation?"

"Perhaps, but I didn't lose it, that's the point. Anyway," he said assuming I was messing with him and wouldn't actually take his money, "we can do it half and half, I don't mind. It's good enough I won."

"Alright then. You can round it down to seven hundred if it's easier."

"No, your half is seven fifty, so seven fifty is what you get."

His voice reverted to a resentful tone. When he returned with the money, I gave up the charade, although I could have kept it up until I opened the door to leave, and then hand it back to him. Admittedly, it might have been risky, so better not push it too far.

"You thought I was serious, didn't you?" I quipped.

"What? Just take the money man, stop fooling around."

"Give me the hundred bucks and we're good, seriously."

"Whatever, here's your half. Do what you want with it," he said laying it on the table.

"Can't a man make a joke anymore? Here, I'll take two fifty, as we agreed. There's no rule about any subsequent bets, I made that up."

"You thought I didn't want to give you the money or what?" he asked, offended by the whole thing.

"Come on, are we arguing over money now?"

"Whatever."

He sat down, as he'd stood up throughout the exchange. We'd lost the habit of having fun or talking about pleasant things and instead narrow it down to seeing each other strictly out of necessity. His necessities, to be precise. However, Richie refused to face this fact, or that his needs reduced our relationship to a mere social game. Simultaneously, it would hurt his pride if I started treating him like he relied on me. I struggled to answer myself why I continued to preserve the remnants of our friendship; deep down, I believed it had something to do with Jane, although I couldn't figure out why.

Briefly revisiting those thoughts, I decided to try to appease Richie and hang on to the shred of comradery left between us.

"Any progress with that online job you told me about?"

"Nah, I've been busy. I wanna do some housework first, get rid of some old clothes, maybe paint the walls or something. It's starting to crack if you look at the corner there," he pointed at one of the corners. Indeed, the cracks became more visible. The thick, old layer of paint had to be scraped off and replaced with a new one.

"After I fix the house, I'll try padding my CV a bit and send it to people."

"Fair enough."

"Though there are a bunch of games this weekend and a few of them caught my eye. Would you be interested? I can offer you some tips if you want."

"I'm good, thanks. I'mma sit on my gains for the time being."

"Alright, cheers to that," he said downing the rest of his beer. "How about another one?"

"No thanks, I wanted to go by the store later, I promised Kim to help her out today," I lied.

"I see. How's that going?"

"What, Kim?"

"No, the store."

"Ah, it's OK. Steady as always."

"You ever thought about expanding?"

"Can't say that I have. I'm happy with the way it is."

"Maybe there'd be money in it. With a little work, the place would work wonders."

"Yeah, maybe."

He cracked another beer open for himself, while I finished mine in silence. Richie talked about the changes he wanted to make to the house and the yard, as well as what furniture he'd get to replace his current one. In the end, I stood up and thanked him for the beer.

"Sure. Let's catch up sometime next week," he said.

"Yeah."

Getting up to walk me to the door, he glanced at the money and covered it with the ashtray, as if the wind would otherwise blow it away.

"I might also prune those trees, it's in the pipeline," he spoke while I walked under them.

In front of the store, the dust, lifted by the many cars and trucks which passed by throughout the day, settled again on the street and sidewalk. Through the windows, both from the inside as well as from the outside, you saw as if through a brown pixelated filter, creating the same aesthetic as that of an old photo.

Inside, one customer was lining his products for Kim to check the barcodes, while two others shifted between shelves. It was 6:30 in the evening, meaning that the stream of customers who finished work had already done their shopping. From this point onwards, the activity at the store slowly decreased until it closed, generally at around 8.

Kim waved at me and I waved back. My hat hid the bruise on my head, sparing me from having to explain it. On the doorstep of the backroom, I mimicked the drinking gesture, to which she replied yes, so I went and prepared two cups of coffee. I drank mine either with cream or milk, Kim preferred it with added sugar. Bringing her the coffee, I told her:

"Take a break if you want, I got this."

"Thanks, I needed to go to the toilet but people kept coming in, I thought I wouldn't make it in time," she joked and darted away, leaving the coffee on the closest shelf to the bathroom. Next, I scanned the products of the remaining two customers. When the latter exited the store, Kim, leaning on the counter with her coffee and a look of relief on her face, said:

"We ought to initiate Georgie into bookkeeping soon, I'm starting to feel my age. I used to be able to hold it in for hours, but now I came dangerously close."

"You shouldn't do that to your body. Just go when you feel the need to, no one's gonna steal from here."

"Still, I'm not too comfortable with the idea. I'd rather wait."

"George always goes when he has to. He takes ages in there, too."

Kim laughed. With her hair held in a bun, she wore no jewelry but looked good in her plain, natural way. She also retained her youth despite turning fifty soon, apart from the deeper wrinkles around her mouth and on her forehead. A natural reservoir of energy, her diligence, and work ethic would likely stay intact until a very old age.

"Yep, George is as carefree as they come."

"Anyway, I thought you wouldn't mind leaving earlier today. Unless you're keen on spending your evening here, of course."

"How tempting, hmm...I think free evening wins this round. Are you sure though? I was expecting to close the shop today anyway."

"Yeah, no worries. I wanted to do some meditation via cleaning. I missed it, surprisingly."

"Oh, OK," she said, with the corners of her mouth curling up and forming an expression of sympathy and understanding. She straightened her back and took away my empty cup of coffee, along with hers, to the backroom. I heard the sink running there for a few moments, followed by repeated rustling sounds. Kim walked out wearing her grey raincoat, equipped with her purse and umbrella. It was a Wednesday, with the Thursday and Friday shifts belonging to George. They shared the weekend however they arranged between them, with me as a backup in case neither of them was available. It wouldn't mean much normally, leaving work two hours early, but given Kim entering her mini-weekend, I sensed she relished it.

"First thing I'm going to do is take a long, hot bath. I hope it starts raining soon because the bath will feel even nicer that way," she said.

"I hope so too. Have a good one Kim, thanks for today."

She smiled and left. Heavy clouds mustered above the store. I flipped the piece of cardboard hanging on the store's door from "open" to "closed," locking the door and leaving the key inside. Then I did a slow round through the store, taking a mental note of what needed to be done. In front of the fruit section, I stopped to notice the ripped banana bundles.

"This is getting on my nerves," I muttered to myself.

I picked the worse ones to take home. My diet almost resembled that of a monkey's, while George and Kim also benefitted from the customers' carelessness. Banana smoothies, milkshakes, fruit salads, banana yogurt, pancakes made out of bananas...anything but fried bananas, because fried things were unhealthy. Thank God for easy online recipes, otherwise too much fresh produce would have gone to waste.

As I began to take cans out of their boxes and fill up a bucket with hot water and washing liquid, I seamlessly slipped into a trance. Richie, Jane, the white bugs on the peach tree, and everything else became instantly distant. I knew they existed, like I myself existed and was alive, although now I looked at everything sort of through a window shop, insentient. It was all there, but I would soon walk past it and leave it behind, overtaken by a profound sensation of transience.

My hands and feet acted by themselves, cleaning and filing up the shelves, picking up and carrying the bucket from here to there, squeezing the water out of the mop, then throwing away the water and rinsing the bucket clean. Subsequently, I switched back on in a way comparable to how consciousness is restored after a lucid dream. The floor gleamed cleanly and the shelves boasted their old robust appeal.

I turned the lights off. The store basked in the immaculate blackness of the night. With my mind refreshed, I headed home. There I followed Kim's example and took a hot shower, cooking a tasty dinner afterwards. Listening to music at a low volume, I fell asleep directly on the couch, where I dreamed of my mother.

"I'm happy you still think about me," she said with her hands on her lap. Her posture exuded goodness and virtue.

"How could I not? You were all I had. It's terribly lonely without you."

"It shouldn't be," she said calmly. "There's plenty to live for. I always wanted you to be happy."

"I know."

We were sat together in the living room of our old house, the house where I grew up. With the glass table between us, the dream combined the physical distance with unmistakable affection, instilling an ethereal atmosphere that engulfed the scene. I could feel a quiver inside my chest, hovering on the brink of bursting into tears.

"You need to break through," she continued. "You have to want more from yourself. The rest will come by itself. It's inevitable."

"I don't feel it in me. I struggle a lot to..."

My body froze, the words clustered in my throat. I couldn't utter it, perhaps because I didn't know how to put it into words.

"That's it," she said. "You don't have to say it, it's enough to realize what it is, which you already do."

I looked at my mother mesmerized by her words and presence.

"You must grow, Chris. Just one more step, then you can take off. You're almost there."

"Was it painful?" I asked her, with curiosity sorely clutching my heart, making it jolt at every second.

"A little, at first. But it's only physical. Nothing abnormal about it. There were other more important things going on in my mind."

The sensation of craving a hug flooded me. The objects, the room, and my mother herself began losing their contour, fading into the background of my mind.

"I wish I could do it, but I can't," she said intuiting my needs. "We are with you, watching over you constantly. Life is too short to spend your time in isolation."

The shapes faded continuously, I completely lacked control over what was happening.

"But..." I said as the clog of words in my throat turned into peeps, accompanied by warm tears trickling down my face.

"I believe in you. Take care of yourself, Chris."

As everything blended together, the dream jumped forward to my grandfather's garage, where I used to play as a kid while he did his work. The garage had a set of steps, covered with pieces of wood, leading to some sort of basement, where my grandfather kept the durable vegetables he grew in his yard, like onions and potatoes. Instead, the dream transformed that place into a pit, round in shape and filled with a perfectly still water the color of obsidian. Now I was a kid again, crouching over that well, or whatever it was. I could sense it was either bottomless, or it ran down all the way to some unknown, abysmal depth. The longer I stared at it, the more it frightened me. I couldn't help but think about what would happen if I fell into the water. As the thought loomed, the sinister water glistened under me. A single bubble rose to the surface and popped. Then I woke up.

The early morning hours oversaw the cold blue light gradually creep through the trees and windows into the sleeping people's rooms, covering more ground as it stretched and changing to lighter nuances of blue, then jumping across the color spectrum, steadily ripening and turning into gold. I witnessed the passing from the blue hour to the golden one, wrapped in my blanket, unable to sleep and deeply forlorn.

It was tiring how the days never started well. Knowing the cause of my existence bothered me greatly, but not nearly as much as not knowing the reason behind it. I could not understand how careless or unaware people had to be to, through their actions, pluck another human life out of the ether and sentence it to potential misery and certain death. That much was unavoidable at least, on my part; I couldn't help that I was born. However, it was unacceptable how a big nothing followed the unnecessary evil. Faith was the only way to achieve quietude, but how could I have faith in the very thing which condemned me to exist? The first thought of suicide brought back the abandonment I felt as a kid when my mom left the house to go to work. Years later, I began to think I loved solitude, though I loved it like an animal loved licking its wounds. My entire life was nothing but a collection of coping mechanisms for that almost ancient loneliness in my heart, a perpetual teetering on the edge of the pit in my nightmare.

I made a cup of coffee to shake off my malaise and moved on to the balcony when it became warm enough to sit there. At first, I continued my contemplation, but soon a strange duo caught my attention. A chunky middle-aged man, dressed in raggedy clothes, followed by a three-legged dog. My suspicion that the man was homeless proved right when he lowered his bag to forage into a dumpster with both hands. Meanwhile, the dog stood by. They must have been companions, doing their daily rounds together. I hadn't noticed them before, since I usually woke up later. Interestingly enough, the dog's missing leg must have been amputated, as there was no stump in its place, only a neat shape marginally sticking out from the rest of the dog's slim figure. The man, wearing a grizzled beard, contrasting to his dirty, sun-beaten skin, found something in there and threw it to the dog, who sniffed it gently and ate it in an almost delicate fashion as if he'd been trained.

Further on, as the man completed a thorough examination, the dog looked at him seemingly with respect. They were clearly attached to one another. I watched the entire scene, rooting for them the whole time. The dumpster lay not far from my store, in fact merely a minute away, located on the street to the right. From then on, I decided to put the older edible products from the store in a bag and hang them from the container for the man to reach them more easily. My grandfather used to keep the leftover bones from his meals and save them for the dogs he met on his walks. Maybe I could do the same.

The man eventually found something useful and took it out of the trash, but I couldn't figure out what. He then picked up the bag and made his way to the next stop on his route, with the dog wobbling behind him.

I drank my coffee and indulged in the soothing light, with my limbs stretched out on the balcony and my eyes closed. At one point, the phone rang.

"What's up," I greeted Bone.

"Are you free on Thursday?"

"Yes, why?"

"I'mma need your help with something. I'll drop by tomorrow and tell you in person what it's about. It's a big one this time."

Slightly nervous, I tried picturing what a serious mission could look like and establishing how far I was willing to go. My mind drew a blank, I couldn't think about it then. Fortunately, nothing could pressure me into taking a risk greater than what I normally agreed to, so I needn't worry too much about it. Better wait to hear what Bone had to say and decide on the spot. White clouds floated in the clear blue sky, so I filtered everything else out and enjoyed it while it lasted.

Chapter V

We camped in Bone's car while he instructed me. It'd been a one-hour drive. I picked up a croissant for me and one for Bone before we met and hit the road. However, my stomach grumbled as soon as he stopped the car. My intestines felt like they were being strangulated and I couldn't eat. Bone seemed focused and professional. Along with the troubled stomach, my armpits, palms, and feet sweated profusely.

"I've been told it should be an easy hit. The guy is in there alone. I can handle him by my lonesome, you can wait in the car if you don't wanna be there when I do it. I'll call you to help me carry him out then we'll bury him directly."

"Alright," I said.

The building was located at the edge of the city. Made of dark red brick with a fire escape on one side, it was the haunt of a local pimp and small-time drug dealer. Locally, he acted somewhat independently in that he 'recruited' whoever he saw fit, although he answered to some bigger pimps abroad. With regards to drugs, he got his supply from Bone's crew, and that was his personal hustle.

I hadn't yet learned why he had to be taken out.

"Do you ever get nervous before a mission?" I asked Bone.

"Not so much anymore. In the beginning, I couldn't sleep the night before and after. How are you holdin' up?"

"Kinda nervous, not gonna lie. My stomach is acting up."

"Yeah, coffee doesn't help either. But you don't have to do anything, just calm down. It'll be fine."

He lit a cigarette and observed the building. No one standing outside, no one passing by, not even a stray dog or cat.

"What are we waiting for?"

"The boss sent someone to scout the venue and make sure the guy's alone. Not that it would make a difference, only to know what I'm in for. You might have to come along if there's more than one person."

I said nothing. My stomach kept rumbling and I needed to go to the toilet, but it'd surely prove a false alarm if I did. I hadn't had coffee that morning, expecting the tense moments to come. Inspecting the surroundings to ease my nerves, a man walked out of the building talking on the phone.

"It's also easier when you picture who your target is, and what kind of person you're dealing with," Bone spoke. "There's no reason to feel guilty about killing someone like this, I can do it without flinching."

"How come?"

"Well, since you're fully involved in this one, I'mma fill you in. I already told you he's a pimp and a dealer, right?"

"Yeah," I said.

"That normally isn't a problem, he's no different than most of the people we work with. However, this guy messed up big time, and he's likely to get caught at some point. Which is no longer good with us, since the repercussions could affect everyone involved. You understand?"

"Aha, I get it."

"Plus, his bosses aren't aware of his little drug business. That's an extra risk that they wouldn't be down for. Besides, if they find out my crew took their guy out, that could also be problematic. Nah' mean?"

"Yeah. How can you be sure he'll get caught though?"

"Because the guy, this prick, works with minors too. He even kidnapped a girl a couple of weeks ago, everyone's been looking for her. She's probably already been shipped off to Italy or Spain or something, but these things are often traced back when it comes to underage girls. I can't figure how his superiors didn't put a stop to that yet."

My heart sunk hearing that. Of course, it's not extraordinary to hear of cases like this, especially nowadays, although being in the proximity of someone who undoubtedly did things like that regularly, unsettled me to the core. With all the time in the world and a dictionary in front of me, I couldn't describe the emotions going through me upon hearing that. My body froze and my spirit buzzed, condensed into a ball of energy, an energy capable of the worst deeds a man could do.

"So, on top of this guy being a liability, he's also a piece of shit. There's no other solution for scumbags like him."

The man who walked out of the building almost evaded our line of sight when he stopped talking on the phone. When he hung up, Bone instantaneously received a call, which is when my whole body contracted and my stomach started hurting badly.

"Aha. Shit, OK. No, no, I'm good to go. Yeah, no problem, I'll let you know when it's done. Thanks."

I stared at him while he spoke. He glanced at me, surely realizing the state I was in.

"OK, you're gonna have to come with me. There's two of them. I could take out both of them, but better safe than sorry."

He took out the two guns from under his seat and handed one to me. Dumbfounded by emotions and the prospect of murder, I couldn't say a word.

"Everything is under control," Bone tried to assure me. "Do what I do and remember, he doesn't have a clue about what's going to happen. The ball is in our court."

As if guided by an external force, I crossed the street and followed Bone into the building. He stopped in front of a door, hesitated for a second, then knocked. The door opened slightly. A person examined us before anything else.

"We're from Mole's crew, I gotta talk to you. It's about a shipment," Bone whispered to the man.

The door opened. Bone nodded, signaling me to walk in. Sat at a table in the center of that poorly lit, stale room, another man who counted the money. My gut instinct made it clear that he was the target.

"Sit down," the guy who opened the door told us. "Want something to drink? A line?"

"I'll have a beer," Bone said. He probably planned to send the pimp's sidekick to the fridge and then strike.

"You want anything?" the guy asked me.

Seeing I didn't respond, Bone said I'd have a beer as well. I stared at the man behind the table. Lifting his head from the money, our eyes locked. Out of nowhere, charged with fierce hatred, I surged forward, took the gun, and fired it at his face. I didn't care what went on behind me, how Bone handled the accomplice. I fired bullet after bullet until the weapon made an empty click. I used all the ammunition, shooting the man in the face until you could barely tell he'd had one. In the dark room, a black puddle spread over a large surface, as blood splattered on the table, money, ceiling, and everything else, including me. Contrastingly, Bone had dispatched his target with minimal fuss.

"Jesus, didn't need to make a meal out of it. We gotta pick him up with a mop and dustpan now."

Standing over the savagely disfigured corpse, where flesh and bone were no longer distinguishable between them, my only regret was that I hadn't had the chance to strangle him to death. Gazing at the mess, I felt no remorse, shame, or fear of any potential consequences. In fact, I felt nothing but relief.

"Let's hurry up, the entire neighborhood must have heard it, it sounded like a battalion in here."

Coming back to my senses, my lack of experience showed. Confused, I asked Bone:

"What do we do now? Tell me what to do."

"Goddammit, this is nasty. We can't clean up this mess..."

"So then what do we do?"

"Why don't you come up with something,

huh?" his frustration spilled over. I shut up and kept my eyes down.

"Alright, let's focus a bit, we'll manage this. First, wrap them up. Here," he said taking out a full roll of extra-large trash bags.

I looked at the pimp's mashed head, trying to figure out how to pack him in. My stomachache quickly veered towards nausea, and within seconds I had to subdue my impulse to vomit.

"I can't do it, man, I'm sorry. Not this one, at least. I'll bag the other can, but please, you take care of him," I begged Bone, almost like a child.

"Argh, fine. Make it fast."

I triple bagged the sidekick, for the bags not to break while we carried the body to the car. Peeking at Bone, I saw him stretching the rim of the bag against the floor, bringing it down towards and under the body. He didn't want to touch the head either.

"Go see if you can find a bucket or something. Grab those paper towels too."

"It's impossible to get those stains out though. Why don't we just leave them here? It'll be obvious they died anyway," I said without thinking.

"Because it's better if they disappear than if they're found at home in a pool of their own blood. It'll look like a statement, like a direct attack from my crew on theirs, that's why. No one will expect to find the place clean, some barely visible blood stains won't raise nearly as many problems. Any more questions?"

"No, sorry."

I managed to find a dirty plastic basin, encrusted in the filthy cupboard under the sink. Careful not to leave any fingerprints, I only touched the basin, as we'd take it with us afterwards. I soaked up as much blood as I could with the paper towels, from the floor, table, and also the ceiling.

"What about the money?" I asked Bone.

"Well, we gotta get rid of the evidence, don't we?" he said sweeping it in a trash bag, along with whatever drugs he could find.

"We might upgrade your contract after this," he joked. "Forget bones, you're in for a full skeleton today," he made a cheap pun.

Unable to even think about money, I still smiled in appreciation of the effort. A few minutes later and the room looked as good as it possibly could, given the circumstances. The table, however, was cleaner than when arrived, as well as the ceiling.

"It seems our job here is done. Let's get them down, then I'll bring the car over, and off we go."

We carried the bodies downstairs. Luckily, a single floor stood between the entrance and the pimp's apartment. The building appeared largely deserted, hence the shambolic state of it. The perfect place for various pests, insects or not, to infest.

Bone crossed the street and brought the car in front of the exit. Making sure no one could spot us, we jammed the bodies in the trunk.

"Another hard day of work," my friend said, tapping the trunk and caressing the car as he got in.

And off we took, leaving the horrible reddish building in our wake, like a scar or a stain on the earth's surface, minus the vanishing memory of its former tenants.

The sun set early and would continue to do so during the coming months, restricting activities overall and, in combination with hostile weather, confining people in their homes. However, other kinds of activities, the less domestic ones, drew benefit from it. Only a handful of people, for example, still ventured out in the surrounding area of our town on those frigid evenings, especially through the forest where Bone and I returned to bury the bodies.

"We're fertilizing the heck out of these woods," he jested. "From red to green fingers within a single day, how about that?"

"Maybe to no fingers at all if we don't hurry up," I said rubbing my hands to fight off the cold.

We drove deeper into the forest this time.

Bone and I settled on burying the bodies closer to the road since the terrain prevented him from parking the car in the actual woods. Thus, to avoid carrying the heavy trash bags a long distance, we dug the hole near the road. It was a single hole for both bodies, but we made it wider than usual.

Smoking his customary cigarette, my partner told me how to proceed.

"Grab the head, I get the legs. A few meters away from here will do."

Not distinguishing between bodies, I snatched a bag at random, although a slushy texture made me recoil in disgust. The blood of the pimp had leaked and filled my end of the sack.

"Shit, it's like a water balloon. Let's switch," I asked.

"I'm afraid not my friend. Grab him by the shoulders then, I'm sticking with the feet. Let's not forget who's responsible for that."

I duly conformed. We staggered as far as we could, then decided to start digging there. Placing the bag carefully not to rip it open and spill the contents all over, we went and brought the other. Bone's lantern hung by a branch, with the shovel awaiting patiently leaning against the same tree.

"Alright," he sighed short of breath, "make it spacious, OK?"

"What do you mean?"

"Haven't I told you? My shoulder is still

sore," he said massaging it.

"Too bad, start digging. You do the first half and I'll finish it."

"Fine. The shoulder's good, by the way, I was testing your sense of comradery."

"Or rather trying your luck. I think the second bag is leaking a bit, I can feel it on my hands."

"Shouldn't be a problem." Bone isolated the trunk of the car with cellophane before every mission. Nevertheless, my hands were sticky and we'd run out of water.

"Can I have a cigarette?" I asked, even though I rarely smoked.

"Yeah. Just don't get blood on the pack, Bella will freak out."

He dug the first half, complaining of the hardness of the soil. I smoked the cigarette while watching him. Then we swapped, and he smoked while texting Bella.

"Done," I announced to him.

Bone looked at it and gave his approval. Next, we rolled the bodies down the hole, placing them side by side. After the first shovel of dirt thrown over them, Bone remembered:

"Hold on," he said jumping down and cleaving the bags open. They would decompose faster that way, even if we didn't strip them on this occasion. I avoided glancing at either body, trying to forget the gruesome sight of the pimp. We continued shoveling dirt until the pit filled up.

Somehow, the next thing I knew was shaking Bone's hand in front of my apartment building, with him promising to pay me one of the following days. Thereafter, I ghosted through the hallway and into my apartment, washed my hands and face, and absentmindedly fell asleep in an instant.

The dream shaped up nicely, presenting me a sort of panoramic view of a splendid peninsula covered with golden sand, biting into a greenish blue river. The water resembled a stream of liquid emeralds, alternately sparkling in the sunlight. Instead of regular river banks, two chains of rocks like miniature mountains flanked the water.

In the beginning, I saw everything from somewhere above, as if hovering over the scene. Next, I noticed a stunning group of tigers, playing on the sand, in the water, or patiently stalking the fish which swam by. The animals were beautiful and innocent. I wanted to go play with them, but I sensed my role in the dream was rather to protect them. Protect them from what exactly, I wondered.

Violently snapping me out of my euphoria, an enormous creature, lurking unseen in the water, sprung to life and bit the head off of one of my tigers. Decapitated, the body collapsed on the edge of the beach. Then the leviathan returned instantly for the rest of the body, swallowing it in one gulp.

The other tigers scattered around, in the absence of a place to hide. That blissful patch of heaven quickly proved to be a death trap. Helpless in the face of fatality, panic struck me. The leviathan approached a second tiger, who snarled at it to protect its kin. The enemy lay just underneath the surface of the water, clearly visible in all its might. The second tiger fell as well, with its head crushed between the callous jaws of the beast. This once, the monster killed its prey, my pure, beautiful tiger, in a single swoop, dragging its body into the water.

I could bear no longer, so I shouted at the creature. The second I got involved, the dream cast me on a platform overseeing the beach, built into the rocks. Like the animals, I had nowhere to retreat, and now the leviathan came after me. I yelled again to further distract it from the tigers. It floated slowly in my direction, taking its time, toying with me. When it got within striking distance, it stopped and submerged inexplicably, making it seem like it lost interest.

Those were heavy and anxious moments. I searched for a way out, but couldn't find any. Turning back towards the water, the creature lunged a great distance and bit off a piece of the terrace. There was still space left to my right, yet I paralyzed with fear. The leviathan resurfaced, lining up another attack. Again, it stopped for a few moments, enhancing my terror. I looked at it hopelessly, sensing the jump was imminent. One more second, a painfully long, endless second. The final lunge didn't happen because I woke up.

The sudden return of the nightmares surprised me as much as it demoralized me. While I hadn't forgotten them, I steadily became used to sleeping well and waking up refreshed rather than tense and depressed. I hoped the dream of my mother and the one of the leviathan would not mark a new decline.

Regardless, I began my day with unprecedented anger, when it came to mornings. It was, in fact, similar to the rage I felt at the crime scene when I faced the pimp. There was an obvious parallel between the dream, in protecting something innocent from evil itself, and what the pimp had done to the young girls. The thought of a person like that causing the comeback of the night frights had me punching the bed and muffling my screams into the pillows.

Marching into the kitchen without a clear purpose, the leaves of the peach trees shone brightly under the light. The sick seedling regained its health, which calmed me momentarily, only to trace it back to the white insects and the substance in the storage room used on them. Flashing inside my head, the mannequin, the unwelcome guest in the darkest corner of my house. Like the man I killed, I couldn't forgive it for the old fear it stirred in me. Dashing towards the storage, I pulled on the door, locked from last time.

"You'll see what's about to happen to you, you'll see," I grumbled. Back with the key, I opened the door and met the same penumbra in which it nestled. The mannequin, unmoved and rigid, still propped up against the wall, defied my fury. I grabbed it and smashed it on the floor. Sitting atop and holding it down between my thighs, I punched it in its face the hardest I could. Then I looked at it, letting those moments sink in. Next, I battered its entire body, raining blows on its plastic face, throat, chest, and abdomen, causing multiple dents. Violent clattering sounds filled the room, penetrating the door and walls and infiltrating outside into the hallway.

The more I hit it, the better I felt. Nearly satisfied, I needed to go all the way. So, wrapping my hands around its throat, I strangled it with all my strength, imagining the pimp's face throughout, turning purple under my grip. When the image lingered in my head long enough, the chokehold loosened by itself as the energy dissipated, evaporating out of me.

"Good, it's settled now," I told the mannequin. It'd been a weirdly intimate encounter, as I didn't project a hostile response onto it. Rather, the air it evoked, with its fresh dimples and deformations, was that of empathy, like its imaginary attitude encouraged me to take it out on it again when needed.

Realizing I'd better collect myself, I stopped entertaining the thought. It was a one-time thing, the nightmares just threw me off temporarily, and, for some reason, acting that way simply made sense at that moment. It didn't mean anything. Therefore, I stood up, drank a cold glass of water, and decided to take the mannequin downstairs and dump it in the trashcan. If Bone asked about it, too bad, he could have picked it up by then if he wanted. He couldn't expect me to hold on to that junk forever.

Turning around, the peach trees did look healthy and full of promise, standing next to each other in a straight line like a young bunch of cadets. With a bit of positive thinking, patience, and luck, things would return to normal soon, and no outbursts would take place again.

With a clear head, I made the bed, dressed up, and threw away a piece of plastic that had broken off from the shoulder. Then, taking the mannequin to the trash, I hesitated for a moment. What if it took longer to sort my problems out, what if the murder destabilized me and I needed something to help me vent for a short while? Not long, of course, but only for a few days, maybe a couple of weeks or so. Maybe it wouldn't be a bad thing to patch it up instead and just keep it as an emergency plan.

Changing my mind, I did just that, fixing what would have been open ribcage fractures, one on either side of the torso. All said and done, a ferocious hunger set in my stomach all of a sudden, causing me to abandon the mannequin on the floor, with a thick layer of duct tape holding its chest together.

I devoured the food with a voracious appetite, an odd deviation from the moderation governing my life. What felt like a long time being sat at the table must have really been a few minutes since Mrs. Trent knocked on my door to check in on me. Anchored back in reality, I was surprised to see the mannequin on the floor, the episode earlier having escaped my mind completely. Abruptly alarmed that it could seem peculiar or suspicious to the person behind the door, I raced to hide it back in the storage room, careful to lock the door and remove the key. I probably wanted to protect myself unconsciously, as if the mannequin would give away some information that could turn out to harm me.

"Everything alright Chris? I heard some loud noises and it sounded like they came from here," my neighbor spoke.

"Hi Mrs. T, I didn't hear anything. Are you sure it came from here?"

"Not anymore, now that you said that. Your hearing is surely better than mine, but I'm certain I heard some sort of banging. It went on for a while too."

"Could have been the neighbors downstairs," I hinted at the porno couple but regretted it quickly. Thankfully, Mrs. T took it in a different way.

"Anyhow, I came to ask if you want to join me for dinner this evening. I did some cleaning and found an old recipe I used to make, a classic of mine," she said with a wink. "I'll keep it a surprise in case you come, otherwise it's turkey lasagna with goat cheese if you need convincing."

Taken by surprise, I didn't want to commit to anything nor to outright turn down my neighbor. I simply lacked the focus to imagine what the rest of the day would be like, what I wanted or needed to do, or even if I should seek company or take a step back and lay low for the time being.

"Oh, uh, thank you, Mrs.T, it's a...that's a very nice offer. Tempting, I mean."

My answer visibly confused her. I was generally straightforward and unwavering in my speech, probably a reason why she trusted and became friends with me.

"Were you busy, did I interrupt you? Don't feel pressured to come if you don't want to. It's normal to refuse from time to time, just let me know and I'll save a piece for you later," she said with a kind twinkle in her eyes.

"Oh, no, it's not that I don't want to, it's just that I don't know right now. It kinda caught me off guard, it's been a weird couple of days..." I let slip out.

"I understand, it happens to everyone. Are you OK though? I'm here if you need me," she said gently touching my forearm.

"Sure, don't worry, everything's good. But maybe I could do with some lasagna after all."

Mrs. T seemed pleased. I didn't know if I sounded convincing or not.

"Always," she said. "It should be ready by 6, but pop in whenever you want."

"Will do. Thank you."

She left. I didn't close the door until she reached hers and glanced back, to which I answered with a smile. She went in, but I continued to scout the hallway briefly through my peephole, like an animal from its den.

Alone again, an instant urge compelled me to unlock the storage room and take another look at the mannequin. I don't know why, but I did not dare postpone it. As I turned the key, the penumbra unfolded in front of me, revealing its secret. This alien object ensnared my attention. Under a mixture of intrigue and fear, I couldn't resist gazing at it, observing it, studying it. And I especially couldn't grasp what stood out about it, why it fascinated me that way. Perhaps it was its utter lack of features, the mannequin distinguished itself through its sheer presence, unspoiled by any details which could distract the eye from it.

The more I stared, the more it crippled me. The tension eventually led my hand to reach out in a numb motion and close the door. Bewildered, I stepped away and lay on the couch, doing nothing but resting my depleted mind until a jaded Mrs. Trent brought me a piece of lasagna wrapped in aluminum foil the next morning.

Chapter VI

The dawn of yet another listless day found me crouching in the chair on my balcony, my eyes wandering aimlessly, observing the horizon reach upwards as its pale blue chased the sun. The area around the sun was white. It beamed gently on the town, although the occasional gust of wind reminded everyone we'd entered the closing stages of the year.

I hadn't been to the store in recent days. Fortunately, I had the presence of mind to compose myself enough and send Kim a message to keep in touch with what went on there, even if only for the sake of appearances. A couple of days later, neither she nor George was able to work, but I didn't fill in for them, instead leaving the store closed for the day.

Every now and again, someone walked past my building, mainly pensioners profiting from the weather and taking their daily stroll at an hour when arthritis bothered them least. Striding into my field of vision, however, the homeless man with the three-legged dog. He carried the same bag on his shoulder, while the dog's hair had grown and, from where I sat, shone yellow in the sunlight. The old routine ensued whereby the man dropped the bag to scavenge the trashcan with both hands. He stood on the tips of his toes and moved with more urgency than the previous time I saw him. For us, the people who had it good, winter meant nothing more than discomfort and dullness, but for the man with the dog, it meant pressure, at the very least. The pet waited respectfully by his side. Hoping the man would find something in there, I realized I'd forgotten to hang a food bag by the container. Then, planning to get a hold of him if he walked by my building afterwards, I leaned forward towards the outer side of the balcony when I quickly noticed the cockroach taking refuge underneath the railing.

"You should have died by now," I said, closing in to see if it was alive. Blowing on it, the roach barely moved a leg, probably starved and in bad shape from the cold nights. His relatives must have long retreated into the dark musty basement of the building, bound to their confines until the warmth of spring summoned them to the surface.

Why did such loathsome creatures exist? We'd called the exterminator twice that year, but they kept coming back. They spread from the neighboring buildings because our street couldn't unite to get rid of the pest, so there would always be one building or neighbor who failed to take action with the rest of us and contribute to the cause. If the residents in one block accepted the filth, then it affected all of us, we were a community only in the geographical sense of the word. Which was also the reason why people in my building weren't friends with each other, apart from Mrs. Trent and I, the reason why hermits like Ritchie loitered around, and why outcasts like Bone thrived in our town. As long as we were not together in the will, we were tied by misery.

Mad at the insect, despite its innocence, I burst out of the chair, grabbed a flip flop, and smashed it against the railing, missing the shot. The bug found the strength to squirm away, nestling in a corner and then freezing again. I didn't want it on my balcony, but that did not call for hate. Alternately, I went inside and took a jar out of the cupboard. Returning to the insect, I held the jar beneath it, careful not to have it fall on my hand, and smacked the other side of the railing with the flip flop. The cockroach fell in the jar and before it managed to escape, I put the lid on. Once I lay the jar on the floor, the roach calmed down. It flailed one of its antennas as it turned around to inspect its restrictive surroundings and stopped in the direction of the peach trees, located right next to the jar.

"I bet you'd love a bite of those nice green leaves, wouldn't ya?"

The antenna moved again as the roach

attempted to climb the glass wall between itself and the seedlings.

"Nah pal, you're staying where you are. You know what? I might actually keep you. I wonder how long you can last in there."

It might have been cruel, but only as long as the creature had some sort of consciousness. I didn't know if it did, so I took my chance. For two days I didn't feed it, just to make sure it would eat when I eventually did. I only punctured the lid with a heated piece of metal to give it air. Then, on the third day of its captivity, the cockroach received a shredded salad leaf the length of a finger. Suspicious at first, once it flailed its antennas at it, the insect jumped on the food and ate it within minutes. Later, dark spots littered the bottom of the jar.

"Not far off from your usual lifestyle. You must feel right at home now."

The experiment continued. Other than that, nothing much happened for a while, until Jane called me on a Wednesday.

"Are you free on Friday?" she asked me.

"Maybe, it depends what for."

"For going out with me and Soph."

"Hmm, I'll try to leave a window open in my schedule."

"So you should. Soph can't wait to see you."

"She's a sweetheart. What about you?"

"I mean, if you two are meeting anyway, I guess I can tag along," she kept playing, to which Soph said in the background:

"Don't be mean to Chris!"

"Yeah, she's right," I agreed. "You already asked for the car so there's nothing holding you back now."

"I see there's no fun to be had with you two today," Jane spoke. "We're landing on Thursday evening, but we'll probably be knackered, which is why it's better to hang out on Friday."

"Sure, I remember airports really took it out of me back in my traveling days. Give me a ring on Friday and I'll come pick you guys up."

"Sounds good. Then we'll see you in a bit, Chrissy."

"See you, Chrissy!" Soph giggled saying my name.

"Bye lovelies, stay safe and take care of each other."

I plugged my phone to charge it when I realized I was still smiling after talking to Jane and Sophia. I missed them and needed something different from the usual people in my life.

The insect was now facing me. I took the jar, with the roach laying still, and put it in a shadowy place on the furniture where it couldn't be spotted if someone came by and I forgot to put it away. That was that with the roach for the moment. Jane and

Soph were coming, so I had to get out of that weird apathy and welcome them properly. A thin layer of dust had settled over the coffee table, drawers, and other parts of the house. I cleaned everything, then went to the store and sent Kim and George home early, tidied the place up, and thus began regaining my tonus ahead of the big week in front of me.

Sophia stirred her hot chocolate impatiently, melting all the cream and mixing the colors into one brownish nuance. Her blond curls had started to straighten out, either because her hair had never been so long or she was simply outgrowing the locks. Meanwhile, Jane was giving me a summary of their time in Italy since we last saw each other. She looked as beautiful as ever. I couldn't help but glance at her hair, cheeks, or lips as she spoke, as well as losing myself in her eyes throughout the conversation. I reminded myself to break eye contact now and then to prevent a potentially uncomfortable situation for Jane.

"It's raining now in Italy," Soph intervened at one point. "Do you know they don't have snow there?" she asked me.

"I haven't thought about that, they don't?"

"No, in winter it only rains. On Christmas too!"

"That's a shame. How does Santa make it there, does he swim?" I asked her. She never believed in Santa. Jane tried to make it a thing but it failed to catch on.

"I don't think he can, he would drown because he's fat," she chuckled.

Entertained, Jane followed our exchange closely. It felt like such a familiar scene, spending my day with them in a coffee shop.

"How do you like Italian?" I asked Soph.

"So and so."

"Did you learn it yet?"

"Yes! Non è stato così difficile," she said with a grin.

"Good for you, spoken just like an Italian girl. By the way, did you know it's the language of love?"

"Yuck, no, but I could've guessed. It sounded annoying at first."

"The musicality bothered her," Jane chipped in. "She said people sound overly dramatic and fake. Can't blame her, honestly."

"And did you make any friends yet?" I asked Soph.

"I have two friends," she said in a serious tone. "I don't think I want more."

"Why?"

"Because I only get along with them. I don't really like my other classmates, especially the girls."

"Did you talk to them?"

"Yes, but I only like Lucia. Her family just moved to Bari. She doesn't have much in common with the others either."

"Where is she from?"

"Spain," she said. "My other friend is Italian, Aldo. The boys are nicer than the girls, but Aldo is the best. He asked me to go to his house for Christmas, but of course, I couldn't. I had to come here."

Jane wanted to laugh, however, she contained herself and looked at me hinting at something. Later, she told me Aldo liked Sophia, and his parents divulged to Jane he'd already bought a Christmas gift for her.

"Coming home is not too bad though, right?" I asked amused.

"No, I missed you, gam and pop, and the gramps." The first set of grandparents were Jane's parents, whereas the other were Ritchie's. "And I miss dad too," she added.

She drank her hot chocolate and continued to play with the straw in the cocoa on the bottom of the glass. Next to my coffee, a framed photo, propped up on two tiny wooden legs, of Jane, Sophia, and I. That was their gift to me. Jane's parents had taken the photo on Christmas, two years previously. Sophia was six years old in the photo.

"You're visiting your gramps tomorrow Soph?"

"Yes, I'm staying until Friday. Grandma promised she'd make crispy brownies."

"It's nice that you could take the holidays off this year," I told Jane.

"I'm glad I had the chance, a friend at work offered to fill in for me during the holidays so we could spend Christmas here. Her family lives close so she said it makes sense that I should go on vacation."

"Bless her."

"Indeed, she's such a kind and lovely person."

"Mia?" Soph asked.

"Yes."

"Yeah, I like her a lot."

"When we met on the job, we instantly clicked," Jane told me. "I invited her over for coffee once, and ever since Soph keeps asking me to call Mia over after work."

Then the waitress walked by and Jane ordered another cappuccino. When asked if she wanted anything else, Soph browsed the menu and asked for the tea with the color photo, showing differently nuanced layers through the glass. I ordered another coffee too.

"Can we go ice skating here?" Soph then asked her mother.

"I think so. Is it set up already?" Jane asked me.

"Yeah, they did it as soon as the cold settled in," I answered.

"Yay, can we go today mom? I wanted to try it for a while."

"Hmm, what about gam and pop?"

"I'll see them enough when I come back from gramps! And we won't do it in Italy, so we should do it here," she tried convincing Jane.

"Why not? They don't ice skate in Bari?" I asked.

"Maybe, but it's much harder to have fun there," she explained. Sophia was still struggling slightly with life in a new country. The children weren't exactly open towards foreigners, which is why Jane was happy that Soph and Aldo became friends, with him even inviting her over for Christmas. Not that Sophia couldn't adapt, far from it; she was a very smart and charming girl when she wanted, but she held on firmly to her biases and refused to compromise, even when it came to making new friends. It wasn't so much of a culture shock as it was a culture upset, or inconvenience, for her.

Jane, on the other hand, struggled quite a bit in the beginning. While the company took care of various aspects of the relocation process, no one could take care of her social integration. I hadn't asked specifically, although I imagined moving abroad as a single parent must have made it all the more difficult. Nevertheless, like any loving mother, Jane committed to making the necessary sacrifices to secure a good life for her daughter. Not only did it hurt to learn she wouldn't be as present in my life as I wanted, it felt unreal because I knew she was unique and I would never meet someone like her. I thought I didn't hold it against her that she'd chosen Ritchie over me, although it was irritating that she went for someone who ended up being the worst possible choice.

"I thought you missed your grandparents," she told Soph. "And now you want to skate."

"Yes please."

Jane looked at me. More than anything, she wanted to see if I would join them or not. I shrugged my shoulders in the sense of 'what can you do, give the kid what she wants', also signaling her I would go as well. Which we did, once we finished our drinks.

It was still early for people to flock to the rink. Jane and I preferred it that way, whereas Sophia enjoyed the crowds more. Next to the ice was a stand where a man sold warm drinks and snacks, as well as leasing the skates. There was no time limit. Also next to the rink and a booth, a wooden platform where a woman sorted out the equipment based on size and put people's belongings into the lockers there.

"Hi, how you doin'," I said to the man, about sixty years of age, recognizing him from the store. "How much for three people?"

"Fifteen a pop, but this fine young lady has a free pass."

Sophia gave a shy smile and then looked down at her feet.

"Here you go," I said handing him the money. "Thank you."

"No problem, sir. You can leave your stuff there, the lady will help you."

"Thank you," I said again.

"Thank you," Sophia mumbled. The old man's eyes glimpsed with sympathy.

"What are you doing?" Jane asked me.

"What?"

"Why are you paying again? You're upsetting me."

Back at the coffee shop, I went to the toilet before leaving and stopped to pay on the way. It was a good way to avoid a debate about who should pay.

"Here, and don't refuse me," she said reaching into her purse.

"No chance. Don't even try. I promise to let you pay next time."

"Pullin' the old trick, ey?" she pouted at me.

"What?" Sophia tried to make out what we were saying.

"Hello, have a seat," the woman greeted us. "What sizes are you?"

She brought the skates. Once we put them on, she took our stuff and put it in three separate lockers. Sophia ran her palm across the blades to see if they were sharp enough to cut her.

"I always imagine falling on the ice and someone skating over my fingers and cutting them."

"Impossible. But people can trip and land on you if you're not careful, so try not to fall," Jane told her.

"OK."

Like penguins on the wooden platform, we made our way onto the ice. The first movements were meant to recall the practice of skating, then the limbs took off on their own and so we flew over the rink, building up the speed on one end to do a trick or take a turn at the other. After a short individual practice, we did a few rounds together, with Sophia eventually pulling ahead and trying a few moves in the center of the rink.

"Do you know any tricks?" she asked me.

"I know some things. They aren't proper tricks, however."

"Can you show me?"

"Let's see if I remember."

For some reason, I'd been reluctant to try out ice skating initially. I was sure I wouldn't like it and imagined having to forcedly get the moves out of me. To my surprise, the second I stepped on the ice and felt the smooth gliding on its clean, blue surface, I didn't want to come off. On the other hand, tricks were a tough ask for someone like me. Anyhow, for Sophia I made an effort.

"OK, this is how it goes. Try turning your arms and legs in opposite directions. Do it slowly first so you can learn it," then I showed her what I meant.

"Alright, good. Now do it again, this time bending your knees." Sophia did it with ease.

"Great, you're getting the hang of it. Now, try doing some swizzles," I said, moving my feet in the shape of the number eight.

"I like this one," she said.

"I thought you would. I like it too. Now try and combine all those things I told you."

Jane went in circles around us. Taking her eyes off Sophia, she began to speed up and do more complex turns and swirls. She'd used to skate much more than me, and much better as well.

Sophia did as I told her, but fell the first couple of attempts.

"What am I doing wrong?" she asked with frustration.

"Nothing, you're just not used to it. Keep practicing, I can't tell you how many times I left this place with a bruised butt."

She snickered and then stopped to watch her mother skate. Jane hadn't skated in years either, although it took a minimum effort to reawaken her skills.

"You didn't tell me you knew tricks!" Sophia reproached her.

"You didn't ask me."

"Who taught you?"

"I fooled around and learned by myself. It's not that hard."

"Did Chris teach you?"

"Actually, your mother taught me," I admitted.

Sophia had a befuddled look on her face. She was entering that age when children start questioning their parents and secretly wish to expose their shortcomings.

"Really?" she asked.

"Yep. The eights I found about myself, though the knee bending and turning I had to learn from her. Your mother tried teaching me more in fact, but I discovered my limits pretty soon."

Soph looked at her mother without saying anything. I sensed Jane's satisfaction and amusement. She offered to teach Sophia some stuff, so they began practicing together. In the meantime,

I skated around them, enjoying my swizzles.

We scratched the ice for an hour and a half until we got too tired to continue. Without realizing it, we sweated heavily and our shirts stuck to our backs. Jane and I worried that Sophia might catch a cold. Our pants were also soaked from the knees down, thus we changed our skates quickly and I walked them home to Jane's parents. I offered to drive them to the other grandparents later, but Jane insisted on taking the bus. They hugged me goodbye and then, shivering in my wet clothes, I rushed to my warm, solitary home.

Three days passed until I saw Jane again. She'd dropped off Sophia at Ritchie's parents and returned home the same night. The following days she spent visiting friends, distant family, and whoever else she had the social obligation to see. On the fourth day, she asked me out for coffee. In the meantime, I'd fed the cockroach merely twice, and even then it struggled to finish its meals – the first one being another leaf, the second a chunk of overly ripe banana. Black dots littered the floor of the jar. I assumed the insect would die soon.

I picked up Jane in front of her parents' flat. A weak sun spread its light through a thin veil of beige clouds. Jane walked out wearing jeans, a dark overcoat, and her long scarf, looking especially stunning. She grabbed my arm and we made our way to the coffee shop – a different one than earlier.

"These visits, Chris, I wish I could come home and not waste so much time on them."

"Can imagine. At least it took less than usual."

"Right. Sophia is still away, she got off easily without seeing anyone. Apparently, they ran out of Nutella over there, she's been eating a lot of pancakes these couple of days."

"She's indulging in her privileges. It's quite funny."

"Yeah, it is."

"Have you seen Ritchie yet?" I asked.

"I actually wanted to say, but I forgot. No, I haven't. I texted him when we arrived, of course. He said he'd hit us up shortly."

"And?"

"No sign from him yet. I don't know, it doesn't affect me, although Sophia said she wanted to see him."

"He's probably slipping again," I spoke.

"You think?"

"I don't know, maybe. Why else would he not say anything?"

"How's he been doing? Did you meet him much?"

"Occasionally. Except those occasions are

few and far between. Sometimes it's hard to get along," I admitted.

"Understandably."

The thought popped up of him asking to place that bet to have cash for when Sophia came. I steered clear from mentioning that, or Ritchie's promises of ending his four-year rut. On the other hand, I planned to confront him about neglecting his family at the first chance.

We reached the coffee shop. Inside, we picked our spot and put our coats on the hangers there. Sitting down, I looked at Jane and couldn't help but make the remark:

"You've always had beautiful hair."

"Thank you! I decided to keep it as is, I gave up the idea of dying it."

"Yeah, good that you did."

Leafing through the menu, she spoke all of a sudden:

"How's Mrs. Trent by the way? Is she alright?"

The question caught me off guard. I hadn't seen my neighbor since Jane and Soph came.

"She's doing fine. Reading and listening to her classics, as usual. She made a great lasagna recently."

"Nice how she takes pleasure in sharing food with you, what a sweet lady."

"Absolutely. Care for another visit?" I

taunted her.

"Very funny, although we could pay her a visit these days. Maybe we could all go out. Ah, we could have also asked her to join us now, shame it didn't occur to me."

"Indeed. Yeah, we could take her out. I'm sure she'd love seeing you."

The coffees came. Our drinks warmed us up and gave us both, I could notice in Jane too, a fuzzy, pleasant sensation. We talked and talked and the time passed around us but stood still between us. It synchronized with the real time when the chattering finally paused and Jane peeked out the window to see outside was quickly turning dark.

"Wow, a quarter of the break is already over. It's almost Christmas, then the New Year, then we have to go back to Italy. I swear the years flew by since I had Sophia, it's like I've been living outside of myself somehow."

"I get that completely. I don't feel the aging, yet simultaneously I don't feel young anymore. It's as if we're constantly moving towards somewhere, or nowhere."

"Yeah, like forever going in circles. Thankfully, there's Sophia who gives me a sense of stability in life. I can't imagine my life without her..."

For a second, she looked at me and I thought she wanted to ask if I planned on starting a family before refraining herself. I might have been wrong, though she opened her lips and closed them again instantly. She must have thought about me and my future, whether I had plans or not. Knowing Jane since childhood, she likely wanted to show how much she cared, without being the one to bring it up: did I want to meet someone and start a family? I hadn't discussed my love life with her, ever. Out of sympathy and respect, she didn't either.

The conversation steered towards flimsy, more pleasant subjects. She asked me if I could lend her the car that day as she promised to see some people farther away. I said "sure" then she paid for the drinks and we left, arm in arm, towards my place.

"It seems you haven't been driving much, have you?" Jane asked when she saw my dusty car.

"How come you didn't take it as road dust?"

"Is that what it is?"

"No. I seldom need it. Although it does come in handy at times."

"Like now," she smiled.

"Wanna come upstairs?"

"I'd rather make it to the place before it gets too late. Never mind, can I come up for a moment? I have to go to the toilet."

"Yeah, let's go. Here are the keys, by the way," I said handing them to her.

In the hallway downstairs, she stopped and took a deep breath, with a satisfied look on her face.

"Aaah, this smell. I always liked it. This kinda damp scent, like a basement. Reminds me of my grandparents' house. Oh, I really have to pee now."

Upstairs, she glanced at Mrs. Trent's door while I unlocked mine.

"Keep your shoes on, it's fine," I told her as she reached to take them off.

"You sure?"

"Yeah, just go."

"Thank God," she rushed to the toilet.

As the door closed, I immediately thought about the roach; there was no way Jane could see it. I grabbed the jar, alarming the poor creature in the process, with its front legs trying to grip the glass and climb out, and put it in the storage room next to the mannequin. Quickly, I locked it back. Then I heard the water flush and the faucet running for a bit before Jane came out.

"Oh boy. Quite a while since I've last been here, right?"

"Yeah, now that you said it. But it doesn't feel that way, to me at least."

"Plus, nothing's changed," she noticed checking out the apartment. "This place has one special quality," Jane continued.

"What's that?"

"Somehow, it's suitable for all ages, barring some minor changes you could make. I always felt so cozy here."

In the past, Richie, she, and I used to hang out at mine a lot. They were already a couple. Her saying that prompted the old sorrow in me, bringing along with it the notion of how little Jane would still be around before flying back to Italy.

"Can I make you a tea or something?" I asked though I'd finished the last box.

"Unfortunately, I have to run. But damn, I missed your place. Can I have the tea when I'm back?"

"Definitely."

I walked her to the car. She'd go directly from her friends, either the next day or two days later, to pick up Sophia, then we could enjoy the remainder of the month together. The engine started and Jane left. I went upstairs and put a pot with water on the stove, although, while waiting for it to boil, my mind drifted away. Jane's perfume lingered in the room. I wanted to tell her I loved her, yet the words could never come out. Perhaps my mind was trying to protect me, knowing I wouldn't accomplish anything by telling her that, only opening up my heart to then fall prey to loneliness again.

It must have been shame that prevented me from telling Jane I loved her. Why though? Thinking about it, the only emotion I experienced with clarity, without it overlapping with any other ones, was fear. Even in the love for my mother I felt guilt; emotions never occurred separately, which is why it didn't make sense to try to pinpoint them with precision. The heart and mind are intertwined, so, when thinking about Jane, I couldn't ignore the fact that I would have sex with her in a heartbeat, despite loving her in a pure way too. But love and sex, as much as they are different, are also inextricable.

How great would it be to live in a world without sex? I could enjoy all women more, not just Jane, without the needs and urges I resented having. Instead, I resorted to distance and indifference towards women, to cover up my frustrations caused by those deficiencies. Love could have been the purest of things if the lowliest of them hadn't attached itself to it. Given my previous interest, if I confessed my pure love to her, she would inevitably take it sexually. Nevertheless, women's own sexuality degraded them for me, not just mine. The same applied to men. I could not forgive nature for being so callous, nor God for creating it that way.

Upon hearing the burbling sound of the water, I got up and turned the stove off. I'd lost my appetite. Thus, I brushed my teeth and lay in bed, unable to sleep. Random thoughts popped up in my head until they played out and an irrational string of images ensued. I must have been on the verge of falling asleep or somewhat unconscious at least when another whiff of perfume floated over. Then a creaking sound came from the room with the mannequin, as if the door had opened. I visualized the path from the bed to the room and stopped at the doorstep. The storage room gradually lit up and the mannequin grew in size, almost until it no longer fitted inside. It emanated an undistinguishable scratching sound at first, then it became obvious it was coming from within. It was the cockroach, scraping its plastic torso to get out. Then the mannequin started violently shaking, throwing the roach around, hitting it against the walls until it ceased abruptly, along with the scratching.

Late in the morning I woke up tired and stared out the window while lying in bed. Eventually, the matinal needs pushed me to get up. The bathroom was opposite the storage room, so that was the first thing I saw after peeing. The insect had spent the last fifteen-something hours in there, in its glass jar and in total darkness. Again, it barely moved. In the evening, unusual for winters, I caught a fly, killed it, and dropped it in the jar. By nighttime, the roach ate it. The next day, when Jane went to pick up Sophia from her grandparents and afterwards asked if I wanted to meet with them, I made out that the cockroach had died.

Chapter VII

The date of Jane and Sophia's departure loomed close and threatened to bring something unpleasant with it, more than just loneliness and routine. They acted as a buffer of sorts, standing between me and my thoughts, fears, and ultimately myself. A classic symptom of reaching the last days of something, the incoming transition made me agitated. Abounding with nervous energy, I set to tackle some problems in advance, namely doing accountancy for the store, checking in with Mrs. Trent, who I'd neglected, and naturally confronting Ritchie about his own neglect towards his daughter.

As usual, Kim had taken care of everything in my absence, apart from the actual number crunching and paperwork. She'd recently ordered supplies, which arrived the day before I went to the store. I picked up a tea box and a bunch of mandarins for Mrs. Trent and went over to her place.

Walking into the building, I saw a letter on the ground in the hallway. Then a moan came from the stairs leading to my floor. I rushed to see what happened; it was Mrs. Trent, laying down on the steps on one side, with a shopping bag plopped next to her.

"Jesus, are you alright? Did you get hurt?"

"Chris...no, I don't think so...my hip is a bit sore."

"Can you stand up?" I said trying to lift her gently.

"Yes, yes, I'm fine...I don't remember what happened. I must have passed out."

With both my arms around her, I walked Mrs. Trent towards her apartment. I only let go of her once she sat on the armchair, releasing another groan.

"Should I call an ambulance? You don't look like you broke anything, maybe it was your blood pressure or sugar levels," I guessed, struck by how unprepared and unhelpful I was.

"No, no need. I think some rest will be enough."

"Are you sure? Has this happened before?"

She took a moment to remember, frowning as she struggled to probe her memory.

"Not that I can think of. Actually, I might have been dizzy at one point last week. I almost fainted while cleaning, but I reached the couch in time."

"You should do some blood tests. Maybe you're anemic."

"Maybe," she muttered.

"Alright, try to relax for now, I'll go grab your bag."

I took the bag and the envelope and returned. Without having her sit up, I helped Mrs. Trent take off her coat and vest, hanging them up, then covered her with a thin blanket.

"How's your stomach? Are you feeling sick by any chance?"

"No, just my hip is probably bruised. I'm fine other than that."

"Good, then try to eat a few mandarins. It will help with your glycemia."

Like an obedient child, she took the bowl I gave her for the fruit skins and placed it on her lap, and the bag of mandarins on the coffee table by the armchair. Her skinny hands worked off the peel and ate the fruit slice by slice, with a blank, squinted stare.

I boiled water to make her tea. The last thing she needed was a cold. Who knew how long she'd spent on those cold stairs? In truth, she'd begun showing signs of slowing down in the last year or so, with that increasingly common hazy look and confusion.

I sat opposite her, on the couch.

"What have you been up to? I haven't seen you in a while," she asked.

I didn't want to tell her I'd been seeing Jane, whom she knew, and hadn't invited her to join us even once. Mrs. Trent wouldn't mind, or at least wouldn't expect otherwise. Still, it would hurt her if she imagined I traded my time with her for better company.

"I was busy with work and some other stuff. Jane is here if you remember her. Would you like to have coffee with us one of these days? If you're feeling better, of course," I tried working my way around it.

"Who?"

"My friend Jane. You remember her? The lady from Italy with the little girl."

"Jane...oh, yes, the Jane from abroad. You'll have to excuse me, I'm still a bit woozy."

"Of course, understandable."

I went to turn the stove off and put the teabags in the kettle. Then I took the kettle and two cups and sat next to Mrs. T.

"Is that tea?" she asked.

"Yes, it is. It's chamomile tea, the one you like."

She watched as I poured it into her cup. Warm vapors rose out of it.

"I've never been so...absent in my life. Not once. If you hadn't walked into the building, probably I wouldn't have got up. And I'm so tired, but I don't want to sleep. Exhausted, rather, not tired."

I handed her the cup after it cooled off a

little.

"Chamomile helps you sleep. Don't worry Mrs. T, you'll get back to normal after you take a rest. Then we can figure out what happened earlier."

"Alright. Thank you, Chris," she sipped her drink. "By the way, my daughter will visit around New Year's," she said. "Would you please not mention this to her? She'd start worrying about me, which would make no sense."

By the time she finished it, she had already become drowsy. I asked if she wanted to eat and Mrs. T said no. The pain in her hip receded slightly. I helped her get up, still covered with the blanket, and walked her to the bedroom, where Mrs. T lied down on the bed and dozed off almost instantly.

"No, I have to lock the door," she said, despite not moving a muscle.

"It's OK, I'll use the spare key you gave me."

"Thank you."

It didn't seem to bother her being seen in such a state. Usually, she cared about her appearance, as a matter of respect for herself. In this instance, however, life and old age had their say, and there was nothing my friend could do. I locked her door and headed straight to Ritchie's house.

Regularly I would have stopped to look at the chestnuts and how they'd lost all their foliage, which in turn decayed and transformed into a dark brown, ashy matter on the floor. Yet, this was not a regular visit I made out of duty rather than anything else. I was angry at Ritchie and intended to show it to him.

I knocked on his door loud and incessantly, violating our one-minute routine.

"Hey, hey, what's the problem?" he asked half-hidden behind the door.

"You tell me."

"What do you mean?"

"Were you aware Jane and Sophia are here?"

He waited a moment before replying. Although clearly ashamed, as the father and ex-husband, he wouldn't allow me to put him on the spot like that.

"Yeah."

"So? Didn't you happen to save money to take Sophia out? She's going away in a week if you didn't know."

"Yeah, I know," he delayed his answer.

"Why didn't you talk to her yet? In case I have to fill you in, she missed you and even told me she waited to see you. Can't you straighten yourself out for a couple of days at least? Is that too much to do for your daughter, given you don't do anything else for her?"

"What? What makes you think you can talk to me like that, what's it up with you? I was her father last time I checked, not you."

"Then how about you act like it?"

He opened the door fully and stood up to me provocatively.

"Hey man, mind your own business. It's not my fault you don't have a family, so don't come to school me on how to take care of mine."

Seeing him for the careless, selfish slob he was, I wanted to kill Ritchie right then and there. Flushed with anger, I barged in and grabbed him by the collar, holding him against the wall. Which in turn made Ritchie angry, as he shoved me back violently.

"The fuck's the matter with you? Get the fuck out before I call the police. Get out of here you jealous bastard, go start your own family."

Normally he would have tried to punch me, but instead, he stood his ground, gauging my reaction. I knew it was in everyone's interest – mine, Jane's, and Sophia's that I walked away, which I did. As a last insult, I heard Ritchie spit in my wake, yet I didn't look back. On my part, our strained friendship had irrevocably ended.

Even prior to Jane and Sophia leaving, I was

straying away in one way or another, becoming more alienated by the day. Somehow I managed to keep a functional façade with them. Not that I was dishonest or anything, but I was still "normal" exclusively in relation to them. On the other hand, my private reality began to sink.

The last week flew by quickly and somewhat agonizingly. During that period, I checked on Mrs. Trent at least once a day, either by visiting directly or calling to ask if she needed anything from my store or other places. I didn't go to other places but didn't want to ask directly if she wanted help, to avoid making her feel more vulnerable. She never broached the subject of the accident again, and her tone sounded unusually hostile when I reminded her about the blood tests. As much as I wanted to help, I had no right to intrude or impose on her what to do, not even on the grounds of her age and weakened body. Her irritability boded badly for the future. Nevertheless, we all have the right to isolate ourselves, for the better or worse.

With regards to Jane and Sophia, I insisted on driving them to the airport so I'd be their last farewell in town. Jane told me beforehand that Ritchie had called and asked to see Sophia, spending two full evenings together, the ones I couldn't hang out with them.

"By the way, did you have anything to do with it? It seemed a bit sudden in a way," she asked.

"Does it matter?"

"No, I was just curious."

"Alright. Well, it can't have been that sudden if it took him two weeks to call, right?"

"Yeah, you're right."

By the sound of her voice, she knew I'd played a part in it.

It was a sunny but cold day – or a "sun with teeth," as we say in Romanian. We arrived early as Jane correctly expected the airport to be full. Still, the girls managed to check their luggage in time to have a drink before boarding the plane.

"Did you fill your batteries, now that work starts again?" I asked Jane.

"For work specifically, no. I would've gladly taken two more years off."

"And for Italy in general, without the work?"

"That I'm ready for. I should come back incognito next year and spend the entire break at my parents' house."

"I don't want to go to school," Soph chimed in, looking down at her hot chocolate.

"If it helps with anything, I never enjoyed a single day of school either," I told her.

"Really?"

"Absolutely. Many of my former classmates said those were the best years of their life, but for me, the best thing was getting out of school."

"I still have ten years left though," she

grumbled.

"Plus college," Jane added cynically.

"Ohhh," Soph let out a heavy sigh.

"Don't think too far ahead," I said. "Right now it's still early, you're yet to settle in properly. Plus, you're going to see Aldo and Lucia again soon."

"I guess."

The staff announced that the plane to Bari was boarding soon. They could have flown straight to Roma and then taken a train to Bari, which would have come out slightly cheaper. However, Jane preferred an airport stopover to a long-distance train. I hugged them long and watched them worm their way through the waiting line and present their passports at the booth. They turned around and waved. And just like that, I was again all by myself.

The following morning, Mrs. Trent's daughter, Samantha, came by and invited me out for a drink. She'd arrived shortly before Jane and Soph's departure. We saw each other a couple of times whenever she came home, although we weren't friends. However, we had a sort of tacit agreement that I'd fill her in on her mother's wellbeing when she came to visit. Understandably, Mrs. Trent omitted the potentially worrying details of her life when she spoke to her daughter. I updated her briefly but didn't mention the fall earlier, I don't know why. To thank me, Samantha insisted on paying for the coffee.

Later, at home, I didn't know what to do with myself. Nothing required my attention, there was no one to see, no place to go. The endless bleak sky outside trapped me under it, holding me captive with all the boredom in the world.

The peach trees stagnated due to the lack of sun. They were also consuming less water, as a result of their slowed metabolism. Not even they needed me. Apart from the seedling which had been affected by the insects. The other three were roughly at the same height, with healthy dark green leaves; the fourth one appeared sick and constantly sending warning signs that it would eventually wilt and die. The store-bought fertilizer could do little to help. I reflected on it and found a link between the tree and my current state. In nature, it was common for plants to be overwhelmed now and then by pests, yet some of them survived and grew stronger as a result. So too with humans; loss, loneliness, and all the tragedies of life were normal things. Some of us broke down, others endured and came out stronger in the end. In my case, as with the peach seedling, nature had to follow its course, regardless of how I felt about it. Using an artificial fertilizer, therefore, made no sense, as I believed it would merely prolong the plant's misery.

Deep in thoughts, I automatically went to the storage room to read the label on the bottle again. Ignoring the mannequin, I searched for the bottle but stopped because the jar with the dead cockroach caught my eye. The insect's color began to fade, especially on the back. The droplets of water I gave to hydrate it hadn't evaporated yet, while the black dots encrusted on the floor of the glass. Remarkably, the cockroach's head was wet at the base of the left antenna, from where a minuscule white thread sprung along. Slowly, the entire body would be covered in mold. The disgusting circle of life continued, with the roach, incapable of feeding any longer, itself consumed in turn. Though the cycle could not be finalized properly, not while contained within a glass, man-made jar. Not unless...

I took the container and went to grab a spoon, then dug a tiny hole by the affected seedling. Naturally, the insect's body had to break down into nutrients, which could feed the plant and make it healthy again. Absorbed in those calculations, I used the spoon to unstick the roach from the bottom of the jar, then placed it in its fresh grave. I covered it back with soil, leaving one antenna out to mark its burial spot, in case I subsequently changed my mind. Satisfied with that improvisation, I went to sleep.

With the pimp's corpse slouched next to me, it took ages to finally dig the hole. Nonetheless, I enjoyed doing it and would have done it a hundred times over if I could. The sensation of knowing I was about to dump his body and let it rot gripped me like an addiction. The act of justice that no one dared apply before, repeated over and over. The cadaver lay powerless next to me. I dug slowly and methodically until hitting the impenetrable layer on the bottom. Climbing out of the hole, the body had surprisingly changed, and only the face remained the same, that of the pimp. His torso had shaped up into a mannequin, featureless and neat, yet seamlessly connected to the head. The eyes, wide open and glassy, followed my every move.

"Sucks being the hopeless one for a change, doesn't it?" I asked the head.

No reply, of course. Standing above it, I kicked the thing down into the pit. It fell with a dim thumping sound. Hearing that induced an unbearable nervousness in me, as if the forest around would come to life from the noise. I rushed to fill the grave and cover up the scene, yet the hole remained the same no matter how much dirt I shoveled in it. When a gust of wind animated the trees in front of me, masked by the darkness of the night, I panicked and dropped the shovel in the grave, which I couldn't find anymore. The mannequin must have pulled it in and tricked me.

Then it all made sense: like in the airport, I was all alone here, in the forest. Frozen with fear, the wind stopped and the trees relented. The darkness no longer seemed menacing. Maybe, if I focused, I could make it out of there safely.

I didn't get to finish that thought, as the earth beneath me shifted slightly. Right after, a mass of dirt formed on top of the grave, which continued to grow until it crumbled, revealing the mannequin, standing up on a pedestal. Petrified, my will was no longer my own, as I crawled closer to read the inscription on the column. With clear writing, it spelled:

THIS IS MY REBIRTH

A raging wind unleashed upon the forest, screeching, howling, and knocking the trees down. Looking up, the mannequin bent down towards me, making for the most hellish of sights: my own face, decomposed and grinning dementedly at me.

The knocking on the door woke me up. A swooshing noise also came from downstairs somewhere. One of the neighbors must have been working around the house. Through the peephole, I saw Samantha. I didn't want to open, yet forced myself to do it.

"Sorry Chris, did I wake you up? I should

have sent a message first, I'm so sorry."

"No, it's fine, I should've got up earlier. It's good that you came," I lied with a cracking voice.

"I'm not going to bother you, I came to ask if you want to hang out with us later."

"Sure. Do you wanna grab a bite somewhere maybe?"

"Mom is a bit reluctant to go out for some reason, she didn't say why. We were thinking you could come over and have a snack at ours."

"Yeah, alright. Should I bring anything?"

"No, don't worry."

"When should I come?"

"Whenever, really. Mom will start cooking soon."

"Turkey lasagna by any chance?"

"No, we're making croquettes. Why?"

"Just curious, I recently found out it's a specialty of hers. She made it recently and it tasted great."

"Hm, I'll tell her to make it more often then, I didn't know it was a thing. She only made it twice or so when I was a kid."

I shifted my weight from one foot to the other, pondering what to say. Samantha gave me no time to think.

"Anyway, I'll let you be now. Come over whenever you're ready. Sorry again for waking you up," she headed back to Mrs. T's apartment.

"No problem. Thanks and see you later."

I still had to perform socially, somewhat, although those responsibilities would soon diminish. It became difficult to focus on the day-to-day, on the routine conversations with people, on what they had, or more often, didn't have to say. My attention was magnetically drawn inwards and focused into a state of mind, a state of being that constantly sucked me further in. Permanently distracted, I tended to forget altogether about the few tasks I had to do. Therefore, I struggled to remember having to honor their invitation, despite going over as soon as three hours after Samantha knocked on my door. A pleasant cheesy aroma imbued the air in the apartment. Samantha was washing the dishes while Mrs. Trent laid the cloth on the table.

"Can I help you?" I asked the daughter.

"No, I'm almost done anyway. Maybe you could give mom a hand?"

"Sure. Should I bring the cutlery, Mrs. T?"

With a look of indignation, she turned towards us.

"No Chris, I got it. Samantha, I told you I'll set the table myself!"

Samantha played it off, continuing with the dishes. When her mother switched back to the cloth, she gave me a heads up.

"She's a little grumpy, I can't figure why. It's

like I'm invading her home or something," Samantha muttered, with Mrs. T unable to hear her over the running water.

"That's OK," I said, "I won't stay long. She can take a nap later, maybe she's just tired."

"Maybe."

Her mother came for the cutlery and told me to go sit down, which I did. Then she bent over by the waist to check the croquettes in the oven, glancing at her daughter before bringing some forks and knives on a pile of plates.

"I heard you made another one of your specials," I spoke.

"Another? They're not that special, they're just good and crunchy."

"Good and crunchy I like."

She threw a smile at me and went to boil water for the tea. Reaching for the cupboard, she asked Samantha something I failed to pick up. Samantha shook her head, to which Mrs. Trent winced in disapproval.

"Tea?" she asked me.

"Coffee please, if possible."

Samantha finished with the dishes and joined me at the table.

"I thought about going for a walk later and wanted to ask you about it, but we'd better stay inside today," she spoke.

"Yeah, the ground is probably frozen."

"Did you sleep well? You seemed a bit out of it when I saw you earlier."

"I don't remember. I usually wake up tired."

"I used to too. Took me a while to fix that."

"Must have been hard."

"It was," she said, "but it makes all the difference once you sort it out."

"I bet."

"The store must take up a lot of your time. Do you work until late?"

"Occasionally it happens."

Mrs. Trent came with two cups and a kettle and sat down. Noticing I had no cup, Samantha got up and brought my coffee.

"It was just cooling off, don't think I forgot about it," her mother spoke.

"Thank you," I said to them both.

Samantha went on to check the croquettes. Another wave of cheese smell came my way. There were two sauces on the table, one dark red and another whitish, which I soon found out was homemade mayonnaise.

"The older I get, the more I need my privacy," Mrs. Trent said, careful so that only I heard it.

I was caught between them, in a way similar to how it happened with Jane and Sophia, only in less pleasant circumstances. Maybe their relationship would turn out the same in thirty years. In that event, I would still witness it as an outsider. Taking the food tray out of the oven, Samantha placed a wooden cutting board on the table before she brought the tray. She served us first and we waited for the food to cool off. In the meantime, we spoke only a little, with Samantha getting up to play music. Mrs. T. had previously wanted to play one of her vinyl records, however, she didn't find it because Samantha cleaned the spots her mother couldn't normally reach, which wound up as an in-depth cleaning session, bothering my neighbor.

I had the first croquette with the red sauce and the second with the mayonnaise. Mrs. T barely touched her food.

"You don't like how they came out?" Samantha asked her.

"They're alright, but I'm not hungry."

"Have a little at least. You eat like an anorexic and it scares me."

"Listen, I take good care of myself, will you stop bossing me around? You've been doing it since you came."

We ate in silence, staring down at our plates. Soon, Mrs. T lowered her head into her palms and began sobbing. I looked at her, waiting for Samantha to counsel her.

"Mom, are you alright? Why are you crying?"

"I'm sorry I was mean to you, I don't know why I've been so irritable lately."

"It's my fault too, I shouldn't have nosed around so much. I understand it's annoying, but I want to take care of you while I can."

Mrs. T continued sobbing lightly.

"It's just...it's just that I'm so lonely most of the time, and I'm running out of days, I can feel it. I don't want to die alone."

"Come on, that will never be the case. I won't allow that to happen, I promise you."

I watched the scene, fascinated by the realness of their emotions, different between them but complementing each other perfectly: fear and abandonment on one hand, with guilt and anxiety on the other. The two sides of forsaking, experienced at once, with my old, forlorn friend crying, accompanied by the dejected look on her daughter's face. I recognized what Samantha felt, how heartbroken she was. Everything followed its cruel, normal course to a foreseeable end.

We listened to music and ate a bit more, without being able to enjoy the food however. When Mrs. T seemed exhausted, I left, although not before taking a couple of croquettes home with me. Not because I wanted to, but because she insisted. Samantha closed the door behind me, right after I waved goodbye, and perceived in her eyes the same tiredness that, at a certain point, inevitably gripped all of us troubled people.

Chapter VIII

Mrs. Trent's mental degradation continued over time. If her decline had been steady and unnoticeable before Samantha's visit, then it kicked off vigorously in the following months. I wasn't doing much better myself, as the succession of spring and then summer brought about a streak of sleepless nights. For the rare exceptions, my rest was interrupted and plagued by nightmares or strange dreams, often related to my childhood. And, of course, encouraged by the heat, the cockroaches reemerged to the surface.

As for the store, needless to say, I risked falling behind with the paperwork, as little as it was, and upsetting Kim to the point she threatened to quit. Unable to face her, swamped with an almost childish sense of shame, I gave her and George some days off so I could go there to retrieve the notebook and do what had to be done without facing them. When I came back from the store, I went by Mrs. Trent, also out of duty. For the first time, she looked old and unkempt.

"Hello," she said wavering.

"Hi, Mrs. T. How are doing?"

"I'm fine, thank you."

I realized she wanted to call me by my name but had trouble recalling it for a second.

"It's been a while," I said. "Was wondering if you'd like to drop by sometime, it'd be nice to catch up."

"Sure...Christopher, we should do that."

"We have this new ice cream at the store I thought you might like, pistachio with lemon. You liked lemon ice cream, right?"

"Yes, I do. Ice cream would be nice actually, with this weather."

"Absolutely. How about tomorrow?"

"Sounds good. Will you come here, please? I'm not that comfortable anymore leaving the house."

"I'm sorry to hear that. No problem, I'll come to yours then."

The next day Mrs. Trent waited for me with a pot of pasta. She remembered we were supposed to meet, although she forgot about the ice cream.

"Pistachio?" she said reading the label.

"With lemon."

"Great, this will make a good dessert. I hope you're hungry, by the way."

"I could do with a bite."

"Go and sit down, I'll just put this in the freezer and get some plates. I'll be there in a second."

I went and sat down on my spot on the armchair. The sun invaded the room, highlighting the dust on the TV and bookshelves. Remembering to offer my neighbor help, I looked and saw her scanning the counter for something, probably a knife, since she was holding a chunk of cheese in her hand. She used to plop some cheese bits in the pasta and stir until they melted. Now, without the knife, she bit the pieces off instead and dropped them onto our food.

"Mrs. T?" I said.

"Yes?" she turned around as if what she was doing was perfectly normal.

"Do you need help?"

"No, Charlie, it'll only take one moment."

She bit off another chunk before I thought of something to say.

"I might pass on the food if you don't mind. I just remembered I should eat what I have at home so it doesn't go bad."

"Oh, that's a shame. Are you sure it can't wait another day?"

"Unfortunately, it can't. But I can have some ice cream while you eat."

And I sat watching her eat, telling me how she planned to move with Samantha once she settled down at her new place in France. I told her it'd be sad if she left, although it would probably be a good step for her.

"I'm still thinking about it, nothing is certain yet. Of course, I'd come to see you from time to time, and you could come to our place in France!"

I had a feeling neither of those things would happen, but I agreed with her nonetheless, which seemed to give her joy.

The next day I went back to the store to return the notebook. Relieved that I'd fulfilled my tasks, I took a moment to look around the store and check if everything was in good order. Passing by the fruit section, the sight of the new banana bundles ripped up struck me like a lightning. Mad with anger, I broke the mop stick in half and smashed it against the floor until I shattered the whole thing. Customers were passing by the store and noticing me inside, so I closed and rushed home. The fury kept building up and gave way to blind hatred. Why the hell was I going through this again? I tried being a good person, stayed away from all temptation and wrongdoing as much as possible, I did my best to live a peaceful life and this unholy rage returned to dominate me out of nowhere...

However, it wasn't out of nowhere. No, because despite my precaution, evil had slipped past it and infiltrated into my life. In fact, everything wrong with me could be traced back to the same source, whose image was embodied by the mannequin in the storage room. I couldn't afford to lose my grip on reality because there was nothing that could help bring me back; my mother and friends, Jane and Sophia, and Mrs. Trent were all gone or fading away themselves. Alone in the face of insanity, giving up wasn't an option.

So, I did the only thing I could think of and grabbed the large knife in the cupboard and headed to the storage room. I unlocked it and turned the light on. Inside, as quiet and still as always, the mannequin looking back at me. I couldn't do it there, the room had become its own, so I had to drag it into the openness of the living room. There, I stabbed it with all my strength, plunging the knife deep into its chest. Barely perceptibly, the mannequin convulsed and the color of the plastic turned darker around the stab mark. Another subtle convulsion followed. Slowly, it seemed to catch a pulse. Horrified, I began stabbing it all around the torso area until I lost strength and my stabs were reduced to mere scratches on the surface of the plastic. The convulsions continued in the same nearly imperceptible way, although since I'd already noticed them, it created the illusion that they were intensifying. Incapable to see it through, I dragged the mannequin to its room and dumped it there on its back. Before I got out and closed the door, a dark liquid trickled out of one of the stab wounds and as I turned the key in its lock, I clearly heard the mannequin exhale.

I was lost and terrified. Worst of all, I felt stuck with that mutilated monstrosity in my house and in my life. It would have been impossible to go back in there and kill it, or wrap it up and throw it away. A bleeding torso in a trash bin would certainly attract attention. As I tried to come up with a solution, I became desperate; only the face of the pimp arose in my mind. I too was a killer, and that could never be erased.

Distraught, I went and sat by the window. The hours passed, but I felt how time pulsated through me, how the hours were flying by and how the seconds stood still. Simultaneously present and absent, uncontrollably switching from one scenario to another, to memories and senseless images, I could hear the mannequin's heavy breathing every now and then in the storage room. I dared not turn around, out of fear that the door might have unlocked itself. The kitchen knife lay to my left, on the counter. However, at my feet, the peach trees caught my attention. I'd watered them whenever I remembered, although without paying any real attention. Now, the white thread of mold pushed out of the dirt, springing out of the roach's antenna, and reached the stem of the weak seedling, growing slowly around it. Undoubtedly, it would soon cover it entirely. I didn't process the information at all; since burying the infected roach there, it could have gone either way, and it simply turned out bad. Which was perfectly normal; in life, the bad is as common as the good, things just had to follow their course. I saw no reason to try to save the peach tree. Further on, as I reached that conclusion, I lost myself in yet another barren train of thought, interrupted once in a while by the sighs coming from behind me in the storage room.

Eventually, a loud banging on my door put an end to my delirium. I quickly located the knife and grabbed it before tiptoeing to the peephole to see who it was. Then I ran to put it back once I recognized Bone.

Opening the door, he gazed at me sharply before speaking in an almost scalding tone:

"Have you maybe thought of calling back? Or you imagined it's OK to disappear on me like that."

"My phone's been dead for a while."

"Is that really the excuse?"

"It's not an excuse. I haven't been social lately."

As unpleasant as my bubble was, I still felt intruded upon by Bone, with his presence lacerating my privacy like a knife against flesh.

"Can you be social now? May I come in?" he

asked sardonically.

"Yeah, come in."

With Bone unannounced in my apartment, my sole refuge in the world, I felt carved open and exposed. The real shock came when, to my left, the mannequin leered at us from inside the wide-open storage room. The dark liquid had vanished and the jagged torso appeared lifeless again.

"You look terrible, have you even left the house this month? And would it kill you to get a haircut?"

The shape of my hair had long been dictated by the previous night's sleep. I washed it whenever I remembered, which hadn't often been the case that summer.

"Take it easy," I said irritated.

"Are you going to offer me anything? Because I'd like a coffee if so."

"I don't know if I have any left."

"...can you check then?"

First, I had to close the door to the mannequin before Bone nosed in. However, if the stress and paranoia made me sneakier, then they also took away my subtlety, as my moves drew Bone's attention towards the storage room.

"Hey, I forgot all about that. I guessed you'd have thrown it away after a couple of days or so," he spoke approaching the mannequin. "What the hell happened though?" Bone asked when noticing the cuts and scratches all over its body.

"Uhm, I dropped some things on it...the material isn't too resistant."

"Aha, I guess. We can still use it for practice if you do become social again."

"Yeah," I said, focused on getting the room closed and the mannequin out of sight. Doing so gave me a great sense of relief, but then I realized Bone wasn't planning on leaving too soon. As I locked the door, I turned to see him browsing through the cupboards, finding a jar with a few fingers of old and stale coffee in it. Thankfully, at least the peaches went unnoticed. With Bone's unexpected presence in my house, I realized the state of disarray which had slowly come about.

Bone went and slouched on the couch with his legs stretched on the coffee table in front of him.

"Got milk and sugar?" he asked.

I checked the cupboard and the fridge. The milk carton was open but I hadn't drunk from it recently.

"Yeah," I answered.

As I boiled the water and then made the coffee, I could feel Bone's eyes on me. I imagined he suspected me of something, although he didn't know enough to make a clear image of what I'd done. What he'd seen was that I was a murderer, just like him and his colleagues. I couldn't remember what I'd done exactly, only that it was worse than killing the pimp and no one could find out about it.

"I wanted to come by earlier, but got caught up with work," Bone said. "How've you been?"

"Good," I nodded. "Same old."

I could see him looking for ways to extract more information out of me, nibbling away with questions and trying to find a way to slip past my defense.

"Are you seeing someone?"

"No, why?"

"Just curious. I thought that's why you were laying low."

"I'm not laying low."

"I can actually see by the dust fluff behind the couch that you're not seeing anyone," he said leaning backwards, with his head behind the couch.

"It's harder to reach there."

"Yeah, awfully difficult with these vacuums, God forbid you bend over a bit to get there."

"You can clean it yourself if it bothers you that much."

"Nah. Don't get touchy now, what's the matter with you?"

He wanted to play the taunting game, but I was too irked and defensive to tag along. I put the milk in his coffee so he wouldn't smell it beforehand, and put the cup and the sugar on the table.

"What about you?" Bone asked, dumping two spoonsful into his coffee and stirring it.

"I'm good with water."

He placed his phone and cigarettes on the table, not before taking one out and offering me one as well.

"Mind if I smoke, by the way?"

"Go ahead," I said and brought him an ashtray. He took the first puff and tasted the coffee. When he reached for the cup, I noticed the new watch on his hand. He must have also been busy those few months we didn't talk.

"I came by today because I wanted to ask you something," Bone spoke. "Remember I mentioned you could do other stuff too, different kinds of work, not just cleaning."

"And I said no."

"Right. Well, I also told you I'm doing pretty well. Some people moved on to different spots, and I was next in line to fill in. Now I'm basically a coordinator, kind of, and I wanna get a couple more guys in. You know, bolster the ranks, as they say."

"Aha."

"But I need people I can trust. I have some ideas of my own, and the big boys already approved them. They also know about you, that you've helped me a few times with the cleaning. And the takeout, of course."

I listened in silence. Bone had been talking

to his superiors about me, which made me uncomfortable. I imagined once those people knew about you, you'd stay on their radar indefinitely. I also imagined how at that point, they either wanted to suck you in, get your hands dirty, and make you one of their own, bind you to their cause, or get rid of you.

"It wouldn't be a full-time thing where you chop people's heads off or transport cocaine across the border like you probably imagine. It'd be similar to how it is now, with more frequent missions, that's all. I'd let you know in advance and the pay is quite good."

He continued to stir the coffee, although the sugar had long dissolved while looking me in the eyes. His expression and overall attitude blended the friendship and sympathy I once reciprocated, with a cutthroat cunning expected of people in his position. Regardless of the situation, Bone always went after what he wanted. I couldn't possibly imagine his proposal benefitted me more than it did him.

"No," I said.

His eyebrows, previously arched in anticipation, formed an almost straight line when he heard my blunt rejection.

"You're the first one I asked. I know some other guys too but wanted to work with you specifically. I told you, the jobs aren't as dangerous as you imagine. You can take my word for it when I say it's a good opportunity for you."

He went on explaining it more, but my mind began to stray, my energy and focus depleted. Rather than a real person engaging with me, I saw Bone merely as another element in my surroundings, an object pasted on the vertical plane which formed my field of vision. Suddenly, I felt I would soon need to be alone, Bone's company required of me a resource I no longer had. Thus, I had to convince him my refusal was final, and do so quickly. From somewhere behind me came a subtle yet clear squeaky sound. Bone seemed to ignore it.

"Did you hear that?" I asked, interrupting him.

"What?"

"That noise, like an old door, or stepping on a wooden floor."

He listened for a second. The noise happened again and, to my horror, I realized it came from the storage room.

"Didn't hear a thing," Bone said. "Anyway, I don't want you to give me an answer now, because I'm sure you'd still say no. Which would be a shame, so I'll come back later and ask again."

"OK," I answered tired and alerted by the squeaks.

He took the phone and cigarettes and put them in his pockets before downing the coffee in one gulp.

"Good man," Bone said getting up to leave. "The coffee tasted weird by the way, no wonder you're drinking water."

Then he stretched his hand to shake mine and left, bringing two fingers to his temple as a goodbye.

As he closed the door, the faint sound of his footsteps restored my equilibrium. The squeakiness ceased as well. Had I thought about it, I would have realized there was again nothing to do, nothing in front of me to drag me along and keep me going. A few months previously, that notion would have been unsettling. On the other hand, now I consumed my loneliness like I had a voracious appetite for it that could not be satiated. At least, more often than not, this was the case.

Sometimes at night, I reversed back to the primal childhood needs where I craved my mother's touch. The gap between day and night had deepened over the years, as the sun's bright light made me irritable and drove me away from people, while the night made me feel lonely and unloved.

I said it before how as a kid I was afraid of the dark. Until one night, when I dreamed of being in the hallway of my childhood home, engulfed by blackness and with the wind breezing through the open windows. Then a tall, shady figure took my hand and guided me through the darkness. After that, I no longer feared it.

Many times, I felt like losing my mind, although never myself, if this makes sense. Even in madness, I'd still be myself. There was only my fixed, object-like self to be lost, built and preserved for social purposes. The presence of others constrained me and restricted my essential fluidity. For me, social life always equated to self-mutilation.

Talking about it never solved anything, although there had been people who understood and helped at the moment. Words could not contain my emotions and instead went beneath them, in a way. Putting that pain and sorrow into words was like a patch over an open, rotten wound. The mannequin merely allowed me to put a face to the real issue, a profound rejection of the outside, which we call insanity.

I'd lived beside myself for too long, buried under a routine of responsibilities and distant friendships. The first cleaning job, the first buried corpse revealed the peace of death, how it silences the entire world and reduces you to pure essence. Sometimes at night, I hinted at the peace I once had, what we all once had, which went away and left us vulnerable to the decay of time.

Sometimes at night, more often than not, I missed being dead.

Chapter IX

The last thing I remembered was flossing, then I heard the door slamming loudly. Bone must have done it. I turned around in the direction of the noise, but what I saw was the hallway of my childhood home. That corridor always looked frightening at night. My room was barely lit, and glancing ahead I could see the darkness in the living room, despite the narrow angle between me and the doorframe. A split second before a strange shape shifted somewhere in there, I realized I was alone.

A certain part of my mind grasped that I was asleep and having yet another nightmare, but immersed in the experience, I had no use for that thought. The shape stood still, laying its claim on the unlit parts of the house. I had to take action and show I did not allow it to intimidate me. In an attempt to defy it, I tried to shout at it. However, the fear melted me and the sudden knot clogging my throat prevented any attempt at resistance. The only thing that came out was a weak sigh, which alerted the creature to my presence. Then the dark shape, like a furious blur, rushed at me in a heartbeat. Before it snatched me, I already opened my eyes to see the bedside wall in my bedroom, with the shadows of the leaves and the branches dancing in the moonlight.

Relieved, I breathed slowly and deeply and watched how the tree swayed to the gentle summer breeze. I watched until it calmed me down completely, and I was ready again for the sweet embrace of sleep. Before it happened, an eerie creak, the same as before, chilled the blood in my veins, as I found I could not move. Was it sleep paralysis, hopefully? Anyhow, I waited a few long, horrible seconds to hear a door open, surely that of the storage room, and the unsynchronized thuds which gave away something was heading towards me. While I usually close the door before going to bed, it was now wide open, and I could spot a mass of limbs united by the mannequin's torso, making its way over. The limbs, thin and gnarly, moved haphazardly, unable to lift the mannequin off the floor, scraping its stomach against it. Reaching the bed, it stood still for a bit before crawling under it. With my heart pounding, I spontaneously regained the ability to move, so I sprung out of bed and went out on the balcony, thinking I could jump if the monster came for me again.

Standing there, however, an unreal sight disabled my plan. A black, shimmering ocean stretched as far as my eyes could see, with nothing but obsidian-like water and tiny waves surrounding my balcony. The moon shone its macabre light on me and on the waves, which quickly proved to be overlapping layers of cockroaches, scrambling to make it on top. In a moment of clarity, I figured the dream was meant to show me the dangers I faced, using the symbols which marked my life since my problems began. I tried to hold on to that precious thought, I could not afford to leave it in the ether of my mind and not bring it to the surface, under the light of consciousness.

And I was just about to internalize that notion, if not for the thuds on the bedroom floor. The mannequin crawled out from under the bed and now rushed at me with flailing limbs, yet all I could hear was the sound of its clomping and its stomach scraping on the floor, as I did not turn back. At last, I felt my hand being grasped by something cold, crushing my fingers. Then, as always, the dream cut off right before it ended.

When I came to my senses, I got up and went to the bathroom. Multiple physical sensations battled on in my body, and I could not tell clearly what was happening to me. When that morning weakness passed, when you can't quite clutch your fists yet, the icy numbness from the dream returned in my hand. I looked at my finger; wrapped around it, the floss I'd used before the nightmare took place. I must have passed out, otherwise I couldn't have fallen asleep with it like that. The tip of my finger had swollen into a morbid purple, crossing over into black. I unwrapped it immediately and watched how my finger slowly turned grey and remained that way. Even a while later, I could not get any sense back into it, whenever I touched something was as if through a glove. The thought of having to amputate my finger made me terribly nauseous, and I could not eat for the rest of the morning. At least I found some bandages in a drawer, underneath where the jar with the roach used to be, and managed to buy some time by hiding my tumefied finger.

As the day went on, I managed to temporarily claw my way out of the murky malaise in which I slipped and feed myself, then as I set to do the dishes, I had to take the bandage off, which sunk me again. Not long before the sunset, the same frantic knocking on my door disturbed my quietude. I opened and a fidgety yet imposing Bone barged in.

"I need you to do me a solid," he said.

"Hello."

"If I ever asked you for a favor, then it's now. You've gotta come help me unload a truck, then make a short trip to help me transport something. Please, I'll explain while you're getting ready."

Despite putting it like that, it was more of a demand than asking for a favor. For the first time, I was afraid to refuse. The price of his friendship finally showed, perhaps in the worst possible moment.

"There's no one else?" I asked somewhat vaguely. Bone seemed slightly insulted that I even thought about not helping him.

"No, I can't trust anyone else. Otherwise, I would've gone there directly," he answered sharply.

"OK. What's going on?"

I went to put some suitable clothes on for the mission ahead. Bone followed me and told me what would happen next.

"A truck will soon arrive at the hall close to the bridge. My boys are waiting there to unload it, then transport the cargo out of town. You don't have to come all the way, it's just a half-hour drive and someone else will pick it up from you. You're gonna need your car, by the way."

The more I heard the more I wanted to stay out of it. I didn't care what the truck contained, because it made no difference. I only wanted to see it through as soon as possible.

We went to our cars and I followed Bone to the hall. He drove faster than normally allowed, so I had no time to process anything. One of the two thoughts which came to mind was the hope that he didn't choose to overlook the previous day's conversation and decide to take advantage of me based on my helping him that night. The other, the sudden impulse to make a quick turn and speed off away from the illegal cargo waiting at the hall, the mobsters, Bone, and away from my home with the mannequin and a senile old neighbor, away from the store which allowed me to sustain my miserable life and, finally, away from my miserable life itself. As the fantasy faded away, a soft creaking sound replaced it. I knew nothing else but the creaking and the stifling thickness of the night until we reached our destination.

We stopped by the side of the hall. A shard of light escaped from under the entrance. I parked behind Bone and when he got out of his car, I waited another few seconds, until he waved at me to come out. The gravel crunched loudly and, in combination with Bone's hurriedness and the fact I had to walk into a building of mobster strangers overwhelmed me. Bone went in and held the door open for me with one hand, without looking back.

"How's it goin' Chilly?" he asked one of the men.

"Big load this time. Three cars will prolly be enough."

"Good, we're covered," Bone answered.

Five people were going in and out the back of a truck, taking stuff out and putting it in the trunks of the two cars next to it.

"I'll bring my car inside," Bone said to me. "You can leave yours outside, we're not gonna need it tonight. You can go and give a hand with the cargo."

Without introducing me to anyone, or even telling me their names, he signaled someone to open the gate. A guy turned a switch and the thing rolled up. Bone went through the door and started his car. Meanwhile, I hopped into the truck and started handing the crates there to the guys to put in the cars. Judging by their shape, they contained guns. The other person in the back of the truck with me couldn't have been older than twenty-something years of age, although his face, hands, and the way he moved gave away he'd been a criminal for some time. None of them paid attention to me, yet they integrated me into their work seamlessly and moved around and with me as if we'd been partners before.

As Bone drove in and opened his trunk, one of the guys walked out before the gate finished rolling down. All of a sudden, the reality of the situation struck me, as well as how easily Bone had got out of me what he wanted. From then on, it took so little for any moment to be the one to ruin the rest of my life. All it took was the sound of a police siren, or for Bone to force me into that lifestyle. I knew he knew he could, and I no longer trusted him that he wouldn't. An extreme weariness inundated my body and the weight of the crates increased considerably in my arms, as the squeaks started ringing in my ears. Seeing the gate almost closing over the pitch-black darkness outside, I was about to pass out in the truck when the sound of gunshots alerted everyone.

"What the fuck," Bone thundered.

Everyone took out the weapons they had on them, including the twenty-year-old, and rushed behind the frame of the gate. More gunshots blasted before the man outside rushed back in, with his bloody hand holding his shoulder. Then they all shouted at one another, but I couldn't make out what they were saying as my vision blurred and blackness descended over my eyes, and I melted down on the floor. I could still hear the faint sound of gunshots in between the squeaks, which became almost too much to bear.

At the end of the whirlwind, my vision and hearing returned to normal. Struggling to get back on my feet, I saw Bone and the guys walking in my direction. They were dragging someone with them. Squinting my eyes, I saw they were dragging one of the members of their crew.

"Let's get it done and get the hell out of here," Bone ordered, shaken by the death of one of his men.

No one said anything to me, nor did I ask any questions. The twenty-year-old hopped back in the truck and we finished unloading it while the wounded man pressed a dirty cloth against his shoulder. A pounding sensation crossed my right hand, as the pain pulsated along the tendons of my four working fingers. Sneaking a peek at my finger, I saw the bit of skin right under the bandage turned grey as well.

Once the last crate made its way into the trunk of Bone's car, he lit a cigarette and instructed everyone what to do. All the cargo had to be relocated as soon as possible, including the vehicle used to bring it there. The injured man would also make the trip. I couldn't figure out when his shoulder would receive treatment, although it didn't matter. However, someone had to take care of the body.

"Chris, take him with you and bury him. Bolt will come with you," he said glancing at the twenty-year-old. Bolt, or arrow, in Romanian, was used to refer to the guy with the lowest rank involved in smuggling, the one who took care of the local distribution of goods. That's what he must have been initially and kept it as a nickname as he progressed. He nodded, but then did not even look in my direction. It seemed those people truly did not acknowledge my existence at all, which, as much as it should have comforted me, made me feel like that one lonesome kid in a courtyard full of children, which I had also been.

Bone took out a roll of garbage bags from his car and wrapped the body, bloody as it was. The man had taken a bullet to his throat, shredding the skin and the flesh and cartilage inside. While wrapping him up, Bone told me to get the cellophane from his car too and use it for my trunk. Right as I finished, he and Chilly brought the body outside to my car, followed by Bolt, who'd held the door open for them, also bringing a shovel and a flashlight from somewhere and dumping them next to the body.

"Be careful and don't get caught. And take this with you, just in case they're gonna follow you" he said and gave me a weapon. "I'll see you guys later," Bone said and went back into the hall.

Needless to say, I did not appreciate how he handled my presence there. We were indeed grown-ups and the situation took a dreadful turn, yet he could have treated me, if not like a friend, then at least like a partner or someone he respected, as I was there solely because he'd asked for my help. Maybe it would have been better if he'd been the one to get shot.

Without speaking with Bolt, I got in the car. Feeling the gun so close to my body only gave me more anxiety, so I put in it the glove compartment before Bolt got in and eventually forgot about it. Bolt sat next to me in the front, also without saying a word. He hadn't looked me in the eyes once since

I arrived at the hall. I drove to the forest where we'd buried the other three bodies. Concealed by the darkness of the night, I felt secure, somewhat empowered even. On the way, the thought popped up that Bone might have instructed Bolt to get rid of me as well. Not concerned if it made sense or not, I didn't care. The dark brought down all the barriers of my mind and allowed me to be myself, whatever that meant, whichever normally hidden part of myself I happened to be in touch with. I decided to keep a close eye on Bolt. Ultimately, I didn't mind burying him and then going after Bone, if it came to it.

The black contours of the scenery continued to unravel in front of us until we arrived at the forest, with the trees surrounding us creating a tenebrous, wicked atmosphere.

I drove all the way to the heart of the forest, otherwise, the entrance area would be littered with corpses. There, I stopped the car and picked up the shovel, walked a bit farther, and chose the spot. Bolt followed me with the flashlight.

"I dig the first half, you do the second," I told him. "And point the flashlight to where I'm digging."

"OK."

He went and leaned against the closest tree, smoking a cigarette while I dug. After a while, I saw him standing still and not wanting anything to do with me. I welcomed the lack of interaction. Soon I thought of him as nothing more than some twenty-year-old kid who I'd never see again, hopefully, keeping his distance and holding the flashlight as I'd asked him. The chill of the forest at night on a summer day, coupled with being finally done with that damned hall and the cargo and the mobsters there, soothed my nerves. Mechanically shoveling out the dirt, my mind, now at ease, began roaming again. Eventually, I could no longer distinguish my hands from the handle they gripped, nor the shovel from the dirt it scooped out. They all blended into one robust texture, one repeated motion. So immersed in my work, I wouldn't have minded staying there, or burying myself in the hole I'd dug. I lost track of the depth, and surely I must've done part of Bolt's work as well. However, when the crumbs and layers of dirt, shining wet under the flashlight's beam, resembled the waves of cockroaches in my nightmare, and every time I struck the earth with the shovel, I heard the crunchy sound of insects being squashed. Fearing the creaking could trigger again in my ears, I told Bolt to pick up the work from there. Without saying a word, he jumped in and finished digging the hole.

I held the flashlight pointed at the dirt, although kept my eyes closed to not have those visions again. The sustained stress must have made me tired since I almost dozed off. Then Bolt's voice, muffled from speaking from down there, raised my attention.

"We good now?"

I went and checked how deep we'd reached. It looked like two and a half, maybe even close to three meters, definitely much more than necessary.

"Yeah. Let's bring him over."

He passed me the shovel and for a split second, I noticed he must have thought of a way to climb out, in case I didn't give him a hand. I guessed he would not have asked for help himself. Anyway, I reached down and he grabbed my hand and got out. We headed to the car. I opened the trunk and told him to grab the head. Bolt made a slight grimace when he grabbed his former colleague, perhaps he hadn't carried a corpse before.

"Watch out so you don't tear the bag with your fingers."

The normal tendency is to grab the sides of the bag and allow the head to sink in it, similar to a hammock, to avoid feeling too much with your fingers. However, the last thing you needed was for the bag to rip and let out all the blood and mark the scene. As a mixture of pity and disgust showed up on Bolt's face, he placed one hand on the body's back, right between the shoulders, and the other on its neck.

"Good," I said.

Standing next to the grave, I told him to put the bag down and help me roll it down.

"Also, always cut up the bag before burying the body. It's actually best to take the clothes off, but this time we can let it slide."

We pushed the cadaver into the hole and I jumped in to cut open the bag. After I put the penknife back into my pocket, I looked up to see Bolt's outstretched arm. He avoided glancing at the body until then, but we made eye contact for a brief moment as he helped me out. Then he quickly covered the hole and we were soon on our way out of the forest.

During the drive back, Bolt remained as silent as before. He hadn't been told to whack me, in the end. Also, I appreciated his distant attitude. All I wanted was to go home, or better yet, somewhere remote that wasn't my home. I dreaded the thought of having to meet Bone again. In fact, at that point, I had more sympathy for Bolt than Bone, if that could be called sympathy. As much as I preferred avoiding any form of communication, I didn't know where to drop my passenger off. Like back in the days, I had to fight off my instincts and muster the strength to talk to him.

"Where do you wanna get off?"

"Anywhere is fine," he said looking at me indirectly through the rearview mirror.

I drove at normal speed, considering

whether to drop him off in front of my house or somewhere else, as a safety precaution.

While nearing the place where I decided to unload Bolt, the question shaped up in my head as to how the incident earlier could happen. In less than five minutes Bolt and I would split paths, hopefully without intersecting again. I figured I afforded to ask him since we'd been equally exposed to danger. Again, I summoned the courage and asked:

"Who were those people earlier at the hall? Why did they attack us?"

Looking at me in the rearview mirror, then at the street ahead through the windshield, he said calmly:

"No idea. Boss said the truck might've been followed here. Probably the Spaniards knew about the shipment and wanted to snatch it."

There were more things I could have asked him: how many they were, did any of them get hurt, would they attack again soon, what if they followed Bone and the crew as they transported the cargo, and so on. However, those questions were all ultimately pointless, and every answer would call for yet another question. So, I asked a final standalone question, albeit equally pointless.

"You ever been in a shootout before?", to which Bolt answered simply:

"No."

Moments later he indicated to me where to stop, which was close to the spot I already had in mind. Bolt got out, said good night in a plain tone, closed the door, and quickly moved away.

The walls of my apartment building swarmed with cockroaches. I approached to check if they were coming through the basement window or the spouts of the rain gutters. It must have been both, with the bird droppings underneath the gutters and on the roof attracting them there. When I moved close to them, their backs reflected the yellow street light. The ones right under the snout remained shady and still. I fantasized about them forming one single mass, an organism which I could plunge a knife into and kill for good. One of them crawled near my foot. I stepped on it, alerting the others and causing them to scamper around, hiding up in the gutter. A short while later, their antennas slowly crept out again.

I went upstairs, unsure whether to do something about it or not. When the automatic light turned on in my hallway and I saw the roach on the wall next to my door, it instantly triggered a rageful frenzy in me. I took out the penknife and drove it with all my strength into the insect's back. Its legs kicked out one last time in a deathly spasm, then froze motionless. I went inside, ran the penknife under the faucet to wash off the white contents of the roach, and looked for the Raid can in the storage room. Through the scratches and the gaping holes in the mannequin's torso, the plastic seemed to have changed its color. Having left it to die there, it now had the morbid grey nuance of my finger. I was angry at it but not as angry as at the pest overtaking my building. I quickly spotted the Raid and would have rushed downstairs, had the can not been empty. The thought of the cockroach genocide and of putting out an entire colony, however, held something which I could not do without, it offered the chance of gaining relief, in a way. Kim had surely set up the alarm at the store, so I could not go there to get more insecticide. There was no other option than to ask Mrs. Trent to give me hers, despite it being a lot past midnight.

I went over and knocked on her door until she answered.

"Who is it?" I heard a weak, shabby voice from behind the door.

"It's me, Chris."

She said nothing and didn't open the door.

"Sorry for bothering you so late, but do you have any insecticide Mrs. T? I have cockroaches in my apartment again," I made up.

Again, nothing happened. I took a step away and looked straight at the peephole, so she could recognize me. Finally, she cracked open the door a tiny bit.

"Can I help you?" she said hidden behind it.

"I'm really sorry Mrs. T, but do you have any insect solution I could use, like Raid or something? I'm having a problem at my place."

"Wait here," she said and locked the door. She'd spoken with an empty voice, cautious as if we were perfect strangers and had never met before. Eventually, she returned. My neighbor must have looked at me once more through the peephole to make sure I wasn't in fact a robber or anything like that. Then Mrs. Trent opened the door and held out the can with her shaky hand. I took it gently and thanked her.

"Chris," she said suddenly, seemingly just remembering my name.

"Yes, Mrs. T?" I asked, surprised since I didn't expect any more personal exchanges between us.

"How've you been?"

"Oh, uhm, I'm good. The cockroaches came out again," although they'd been out for months.

"Yes, they come out in the summer. I hope it's nothing serious," she said about the supposed problem in my apartment.

"No, this should sort it out. Did I wake you up?"

Both our personal issues reverted our relationship back to when we first met and barely talked. It didn't bother me then, since I was solely focused on killing as many cockroaches as possible. On the other hand, Mrs. Trent had the air of someone who'd recently woken up out of a coma.

"No, Chris," she obviously lied. "Don't worry."

"I'll bring it back later," I told her.

"It's alright, keep it. I'll get a new one next time I go out."

"OK. Thank you, Mrs. T."

I turned away to leave when, probably clinging to those precious seconds of human interaction which took place so rarely, my neighbor rushed to say:

"Would you like to come by sometime this week? I got that lemon ice cream you like, it helps to cool off from the heat of the days."

It was her who used to like lemon ice cream, not me, although she must have forgotten that as well. It sounded like Mrs. Trent tried to lure me in a way similar to what grandparents say when they haven't seen their grandchildren in a while. In reality, it was the cry of solitude and a need for human warmth. What Mrs. Trent needed most at that time was a friend. However, my warmth had faded, and I could no longer be a friend to anyone, not even to myself.

"Yeah, sounds good. Let's do that."

"Alright," with her smile giving away her

gratefulness. "Pop in whenever you want. Let me know if you need any help with that."

"With what? Oh yes, sure. Thanks again."

"No problem. Good night, Chris."

"Goodbye, Mrs.T."

Starting from the corners of my balcony and the drains of the sink and bathtub, where baby roaches occasionally popped out, I went through and around the apartment building, spraying the fatal toxins directly on the roaches and watching them scatter and then, not reaching too far, dying off one by one. I hadn't been so focused and present in months, killing the insects felt like melting away my problems. On one roach, I sprayed the Raid right on its head and watched it run in circles, poisoned and confused, before it flipped on its back and died.

Once I finished with my building, after two rounds of going around and either pulverizing the insect clusters or crushing the single ones, I crossed the street and did the same around the shop. Exterminating the bugs under the gutters or where the pavement met the building gave me more satisfaction than anything I'd ever gained from the store.

Moving from one colony to the next along the buildings, I could not get enough of it. For as long as the can sprayed its poison, I walked around decontaminating the streets, alleviating my mind in the process, cleansing it of the blots infesting my subconscious like scores of black pustules. I managed to reach the end of the street before running out of spray. Behind me, multiple trails of bodies, most of them dead, others trying to grab a hold of the air to roll over and save themselves.

The town was quiet, covered by the summer night like a warm blanket. A gentle breeze softly caressed my skin every now and then. I found myself briefly floating in the dream that life used to be before evil seeped in and I fell within myself.

Making the slow walk home, I noticed all the roaches had died by then. In the beginning, I took control and dominated the street, conducting my assault with energy and purpose, but the silent calmness afterwards made me feel like a child again. The buildings seemed so tall and imposing around me, although sort of protective in a way, similar to a nest holding its hatchlings.

For the rest of the night, until I fell asleep, my mind drew a blank, yet in the most restful manner possible. It'd been too long since it had last given me any sort of respite. Tired and soothed, I went to bed and, finally, slept a dreamless sleep.

Chapter X

The next days passed quietly with no news from Bone or anyone else for that matter. Inconveniently, when all the food ran out, I had to go out and buy some. I went to a different store, the one I'd been going to for the last couple of months, to avoid running into Kim and George. Then, on one of those precious few days of rest, I mobilized myself and went to see Mrs. Trent, as promised.

I waited a long time at the door before she opened it. After she convinced herself it was safe to allow me in the house, my neighbor's affection for me suddenly rekindled.

"What can I get you my dear?" she asked. "Oh, you won't guess what I have here for you," she quickly continued. Then she took out the lemon ice cream from the freezer, happy as if she'd bought her grandson his favorite sweets.

"Yeah, that's the good one," I played along. "I'll have a coffee, thank you."

Delighted, she filled up the kettle and turned on the gas stove. I hadn't been in her house recently, so I was surprised to see how uncommonly messy it was, for her standards. A dirty pile of dishes racked up in the sink, with the bottle of dishwashing liquid lying slimy and empty on the side. Mrs. Trent worked around them, seemingly unbothered. Also, since she'd been hiding behind her door every time we'd last spoken, I got to notice that she'd hunched over slightly. Her steps lost their easiness, with my neighbor now stomping the floor when walking. However, perhaps the worst thing of all, the entire apartment smelled stale, with Mrs. Trent herself emanating a slight scent of unwashed clothes and urine. At the moment, I felt disgust rather than pity.

"Have you talked to Samantha recently?" she asked from the kitchen.

"No, I haven't." We weren't friends and only spoke when she came to visit, which Mrs. Trent knew, or used to know. "Have you?" I asked back.

"No. She hasn't called in a while."

"Maybe she's busy. You can call her though."

"Maybe, but I think she should call me first."

"Did Samantha find a house yet? She wants to move away from Paris, right?"

"Paris...? Oh yes, my husband is helping her look for a place in France, somewhere in the countryside. Or so I hope, I don't want to go over to a big city to visit her. I've always been one for more rural areas."

"Your husband?"

"Yes, he went over to help her look. Or...oh."

She switched her focus on the kettle, picking it up with a towel around the handle and pouring the water in her teacup and into the coffee press. All the while, her frowned eyebrows and the grimace on her face indicated how stressed she was, and how difficult everyday tasks had become.

At last, she left the kettle next to the overloaded sink and made her way over, careful not to spill anything. I offered to take the coffee from her hand, to which she answered with a scowl.

"Thank you," I said once she put the cup on the table. Through the tinted glass, the coffee looked transparent and weird, like stirred water in a dirty pool. I used my lips to feel the temperature of the drink without tasting it. Surely without meaning it, Mrs. Trent served me a cup of lukewarm, uninfused coffee.

"I forgot about cream, but I don't think I have any, to be honest," she said.

"It's alright. I have a stomachache anyway, so I might not be able to drink it all."

"Should I get you some medicine?"

"No, it'll go away by itself. Thank you."

She took a sip from her mug and made a disgruntled face. Her tea was cold and tasteless too.

"They don't make teas like they used to. It's all these processes they use nowadays to dry the herbs, and the coloring and preservatives as well. We used to have a lovely little natural shop where we lived in France, with all sorts of herbal teas. That was the best tea I ever had."

"I see."

"You don't even like tea. But they also had coffee, they brought it from all over the world. Brazil, the Ivory Coast, they had everything. You would have loved it."

I smiled at her. Shortly I realized we had nothing to talk about anymore. She'd turned into one of those old people who you'd let talk about whatever they wanted while counting how many minutes were left before you could leave.

"The other day I went to buy groceries and picture this, I couldn't find the shop! I've never had that happen to me before," my neighbor spoke.

"What do you mean you couldn't find it? Didn't you go to my store?"

"Your store? What are you talking about? I went to the one by the park, I was looking for a specific cooking cream you can only find there."

Then I asked which cooking cream she meant since I knew the one she generally used. She confirmed it was the very same.

"We have that at the store as well. At least you probably had a nice walk to that other place," I said.

She looked at me bemused.

"Your store…?"

"Yeah, across the street from here."

Then her face lit up.

"Oh yes, of course! Honestly, I didn't even think about going there. But maybe I should have because after I finished shopping, I forgot a bag there, so I had to go all the way back to get it. It can be quite effortful at times, being old," Mrs. Trent chuckled.

"Back when Samantha was here you were talking about moving in with her, am I right?"

"I don't remember. Was I?"

"I believe so."

"Well, that wouldn't make any sense. I'm going to live here with my husband after he comes back."

She drank the tea and made a face again. I looked around the house, without her observing me. The plants on the top shelves drooped down, dried out, and were almost dead. The way the sun shone highlighted the side of the painting's frame, covered by a grey layer of dust. The apartment, along with Mrs. Trent herself, suffered from a prolonged period of neglect. She either overlooked it or could simply not take proper care anymore. The tired, tainted skin of her face, stretched out and hanging under her eyes and chin, almost glued to her skull, attested to her deplorable state. I'd been studying it, fascinated by how easily people can degrade, and the thin thread by which our wellbeing hangs. Every time she mentioned her husband, she then scanned the surroundings with confusion, struggling to regain her bearings. I didn't say anything about her husband. It made no sense to disrupt her.

"Why did you ask?" she went back to my question.

"Ask what?"

"About moving in with my daughter?"

"No reason. Just curious."

"It seemed like a suggestion more than a question."

Which it was, but I didn't want to have that conversation with her.

"I didn't mean it like that. Why would I suggest that?"

"I don't know. You should know," she said slightly upset.

"I don't. Honestly, I only wanted to catch up with you Mrs. T. It's been a while, and these were some difficult months for me."

"How come?"

"Been busy with work and stuff...would you like some ice cream? I've been thinking about it for a while now," I changed the subject.

"Oh yes, definitely. You won't guess which one I have," and the childish pleasure reemerged on her face.

"Hmm, the dark chocolate one?"

"No, no, it's your favorite one," she said with even more satisfaction.

"Lemon?"

"Yes!"

"Really? Let me get it then."

I went and put it in bowls. Only one was clean and ready to be used, so I washed another one from the sink and went back with the ice cream.

All throughout eating it, Mrs. Trent jumped from one facial expression to another. She no longer kept track of herself or how she appeared to others. She flipped between emotions, although overall she seemed lost. Largely incompetent, her behavior had become riddled with immature bursts and quiet periods in which she stared ahead at nothing in particular, followed by sneaky strange glances. We both ate slowly, but for different reasons. For a change, I was concerned about what to do with her and how to help her without spending too much time together. Soon, at around 6'oclock, my neighbor suddenly grew tired.

"Thank you for everything Mrs. T," I said when she yawned a second time.

"Are you going home?"

"Yes, it's getting late soon."

"OK."

I took away the dishes, since she appeared lost again, and washed some plates and bowls, although not all of them. She said nothing while I did it.

"Is your phone charged, by the way?" an idea came to my head.

"I don't know," she muttered.

I checked. It wasn't, so I plugged it in for a couple of minutes. Then I turned it on, entered the default PIN code '0000', and waited for notifications to show up. Instantly, I saw there had been more than twenty missed calls from Samantha in the previous three days. I sent her a message from my phone saying everything was alright and that I would call her in a few minutes. Then I put Mrs. T to bed and locked the door from the outside with my spare key.

Not a minute passed since walking into my apartment when Samantha called me. As soon as I found myself alone again, my empathy and drive to do good for others waned. I let the phone ring, tempted to turn it off once it stopped. However, a pang of gnawing guilt made me pick up, perhaps the only emotion from my past which endured and stayed with me.

"Hi Chris, I just saw the message. Can you talk? Sorry, but I had to call you, I couldn't wait any longer, I'm worried sick about mom. Is she OK?"

Samantha's voice came across as strained from the desperation which must have come over her. It tamed my impulses since I could relate to it. Because of that, I actually wanted to help her.

"Yes, I've just come back from her place. Her phone had died and she didn't charge it."

"Thank God! There was no way to reach her, I almost booked a ticket there. It didn't even cross my mind to call you."

"She's sleeping now, but you can call her later. I plugged in her phone so it should stay turned on."

"Thank you so much for checking. How come she didn't think about it earlier, I call her at least twice a week."

"I've no idea. Well, not to alarm you or anything, but she doesn't seem herself lately..."

"What do you mean?"

With the initial desperation now behind her, a familiar sort of tension set in her voice. It was the anticipation of the inevitable, the moment when the ticking of the clock stops, ending the long nervous wait for the heartbreak to happen. The only good news about old loved ones is no news at all.

I filled her in on Mrs. Trent's difficulties, from keeping the apartment clean to the increasing episodes of confusion and irritation, as well as her short-term memory issues. I didn't mention the hunch, poor hygiene, or that she repeatedly brought up her dead husband. Samantha had enough on her plate for the time being.

She received that information well, meaning that she must have braced herself for an outcome like that.

"Just to get an idea, has this gradually got worse since I last saw her?" she asked.

"Yes, it has."

"Then it's pretty clear what it is," she said dejectedly. "I imagined it wouldn't be the case with her. I mean it's obvious she wouldn't be the same now as she was thirty years ago. She's a smart, educated woman, she took good care of herself, continued reading, and kept her mind sharp...I really hoped it wouldn't come to this."

Later I thought how remorse would flood Samantha like never before, as it does with all people who aren't able to look out after their aging parents, for one reason or another. In Samantha's case, the distance between her and Mrs. Trent, which resulted from Samantha's decision to live away from her mother – which is not always a damning factor, as Samantha had to pursue the best life for herself – exacerbates the child's guilt. Even if not justified, Samantha would still feel like a horrible daughter to Mrs. Trent.

I understood her too well. And I appreciated that she didn't ask me to keep an eye out on her mother until she managed to book a plane ticket.

However, I consciously avoided offering to take care of Mrs. Trent until Samantha arrived, which would likely be in around two weeks. She thanked me again and I promised to keep her updated. Then she hung up.

The evening coated the town with its obscurity. The drapes of darkness seamlessly drew over my windows, sucking the life out of my apartment. My descent set off again, as I withstood the endless polar-like nights. There were only two distinct points in time, coinciding with the vexing, hazy light of day, or with the impenetrable blackness, and I was stuck in both respectively. The uninterrupted cycle of day and night can be truly maddening for a person already struggling to find stability.

Curled up on the couch and going through the motions, I did not realize that Ritchie texted. He asked about me and wanted to meet whenever possible to clarify things. I no longer had the energy to spare on a friendship with him, so I did not text back.

Following an initial relief of somewhat fulfilling my duty towards Mrs. Trent by signaling her problems to someone else, my thoughts regressed towards guilt. The image of Mrs. Trent living alone yet so close to me, merely separated by a couple of walls, incapably stumbling around the house and prone to self-harm and depression, cast me even further down.

Dispirited and exhausted, I continued to fall asleep and wake up on the couch, as held down by an unseen weight. The same nightmare took place over and over, in which I saw Mrs. Trent sitting in a brightly lit asylum room, wearing a clean white robe contrasting with her grey skin, the same nuance as my finger, and with her arms cut beneath the shoulders. With the confused, slightly scared look on her face from my visit beforehand, I woke up every time she opened her mouth to ask for help. When the blue of dawn cracked the night outside, I managed to drag myself to the bedroom and slipped into a heavy slumber.

I woke up in the afternoon with my hands shaking and my head throbbing. In the past two days, I'd eaten nothing apart from a bowl of lemon ice cream which, adding to the months of poor sleep, resulted in a splitting headache. All in all, my neighbor and I were facing similar difficulties. The near future held no promise of a change in fortune. So, to make things easier for myself, I texted Kim and told her I wanted to talk about the situation with the store. We met after the closing hour, with no one else there. It still caused me a great amount of stress, especially the instant we saw each other. She kept up the implacable expression on her face throughout the conversation, which lasted little but felt drawn out and uncomfortable. Essentially, I tried to apologize and offer her all the profit from the store in exchange for her taking care of everything, from cleaning, selling, ordering products, and doing the bookkeeping for as long as necessary. She asked why, to which I told her I'd been having some personal problems and would rather not go into details. She appeared to soften after that, and offered to do all those things for no extra money. Eventually we agreed on a salary raise, once I specified that those problems could go on for a while. Kim also offered to help on a personal level, or at least keep me company in case I needed to talk to someone. I thanked her deeply and trudged back home, humbled by her kindness, after remembering to grab some food so I wouldn't starve to death.

I'd lost track of the days, but I knew it was early August. The beginning and end of summer were easy to distinguish, but the middle always went by irritatingly slowly and buried me under its hot, tedious days. The present seemed so unnavigable that I couldn't picture what the future would be like. Still, at least some things had to repeat themselves. Some loops cannot be stopped. Jane and Sophia would come to visit again, perhaps even sometime soon; I would have to go buy food and meet Kim eventually as well; Samantha had already said she would fly over shortly; I would have to see Mrs. Trent at least one more time and say goodbye, and so on...

The second I unpacked what I'd brought from the store, my famished body started overloading my brain with signals, as a dull ache settled in my stomach and a fainting sensation tested my strength constantly. Even as I finished eating, the pain persisted until much later. I sat in the chair and clutched my stomach for a while, staring out the window with a quiet mind. Of the four peach trees, two still remained somewhat intact. One had been consumed until it dried up and became a brown stump, while the one next to it, the second in line to be infected, turned into a fuzzy statuette of white and blue mold. The two peach seedlings on the right were far away enough not to contact the disease. Unaware of it, I must have watered them occasionally, otherwise they would have died by now. My apartment and I formed some sort of symbiosis, and were both like an abandoned garden, with the overgrown weeds consisting of the parasitic thoughts cluttering in my head. I knew it couldn't have lasted, but the brief period of respite had undoubtedly reached its end.

Chapter XI

The grey robust walls flanked the wide hallway, with the floor tiles reflecting back the strong light coming through the barred windows. People were ghosting by without acknowledging me. I went to the last room at the end of the hallway. No one walked in or out of there apart from me. A blue, morgue-like light filled the space there, different from the pleasant one in the rest of the building. The solitary figure sitting in front of the window split the incoming stream of light in two. Matching the color of the walls, she had long white hair and wore a white robe. However, when I got closer to her, the color of her skin struck me. It was a morbid grey, riddled with creases and it revealed the terrible amount of pain and neglect the person had been through.

Hearing my footsteps, the woman sat up and turned around. Until that point, I believed she'd kept her hands in her lap; however, they were missing nearly entirely, bar the scarred stumps above the elbows. Mrs. Trent appeared to be just as scared as I was. Her lip quivered as she tried to talk. I couldn't say anything either because of the shock.

That nightmare caught me off guard whenever I had it. I never recognized the hallway, the light, the walls, or the person by the window in the last room, until she turned around. Then we stared at each other, both of us unable to communicate. Then, before she finally managed to ask for help, the dream finished abruptly.

So it did one night, and I woke up as usual. On the wall to the right of the bed, the leaves and branches carried out their dance in the moonlight. I tried to move towards the window to look at them, although I couldn't control my body. All I could do was blink and roll my eyes. At first, I panicked but then I recognized that it must have been sleep paralysis, so I did my best to remain calm. Which worked until a quiet creak came from afar. I could only glance at the doorframe and not beyond that. The creak happened again, this time closer and a bit louder, then again, even louder, and went on until it stopped entirely. Conflicted between confirming my suspicion or ignoring what caused those sounds in the hope it'd go away, I painfully rolled my eyes down as much as possible to see the mannequin standing in the doorframe in plain sight. It stared at me with its eyeless face, and I stared back terrified and with ice bursting through my veins. In the absolute tension, our gazes remained locked until the light of day seeped through the windows. Then, unaware of what happened, whether I passed out or gave in to delirium, I suddenly regained focus but the mannequin disappeared.

The loud sound of the banging door got me out of bed and fully alert. I popped my head around the corner to see the door to the storage room closed and the key in the lock. To the right, the bathroom was open with no one in there. The sound must have come either from the hallway or the balcony, I thought. Then, turning the next corner and walking into the kitchen, I found myself staring into the barrel of a black gun, pointed straight at my face. Behind the weapon was a dark hooded, masked silhouette. He said nothing but pointed the weapon at me. Then the man took down the mask and hoodie and grinned cynically at me.

"You stopped locking your door now? Not the smartest move if you ask me."

Bone put the gun under his belt and went to sit down on the couch.

"Was it open?" I asked him.

"No, I picked your lock. Yeah, of course it was open. You didn't seem too bothered about the piece though. Did you recognize me or what?"

The sight of the gun stunned me, obviously. However, I didn't fear for my life or anything. Probably, if I had time to think about it, there were worse things that could happen to me other than being killed. More than anything, an armed stranger was just more trouble to deal with.

Also, the discussion with Bone slipped my mind altogether since I'd gone to help him at the hall. The issue of ending our partnership appeared to have resolved itself. However, his unexpected and unwelcome presence around me put brought up that problem, and now it needed to be sorted out for good. I had to tell him clearly that we could no longer do business together, however careful not to upset him. If he lost trust in me, it could make him consider me a threat and thus consider getting rid of me, especially since our friendship had boiled down to the occasional act of crime.

"No, I just hoped you wouldn't shoot me."

"There's still time for that. Can you boil some water in the meantime?"

"Why?"

"Coffee," he said throwing two soluble coffee sticks on the table and two cream ones.

"Yeah," I spoke.

"Luckily I remembered to bring some myself this time."

He walked around and leaned against the counter close to me, though I moved away pretending to be looking for something.

"Your remuneration, by the way."

Bone handed me the envelope. I stood still, wanting to tell him how much I loathed him and his envelope. Seeing I didn't reach for it, he put it down on the counter instead and went back on the couch.

"Can you get an ashtray?" he asked.

I set the water to boil and brought him the ashtray.

"What's with your hand?" he said.

"Nothing, I cut my finger yesterday."

Then a while went by during which neither of us said anything. I poured water into one cup and took it to Bone.

"You're not having any?" he asked.

"No."

He played with the cigarette between his fingers, then took a drag and blew out a smoke circle.

"I've been away until now, otherwise I would have come by earlier to discuss. So, what do you think?"

"About what?"

"About my proposal."

I made an effort to look him in the eyes so that he understood there was no hesitation on my part.

"No. I want nothing to do with it."

"If what happened last time put you off, just know that it generally never happens. Someone in our group made a mistake that will not repeat in the future. I told you, I'd only give you the safe jobs if that's what you're thinking about."

"I'm not thinking about it at all. There's no way I'mma get involved. This is my final answer."

He put out the cigarette and fiddled with the stub in the ashtray.

"That's a shame," he said before lighting up another one. "It would've been way smoother than you imagine. And it would have saved me the trouble of trying to find someone else that I can trust, while for you this would have been a unique opportunity. But, since you're so determined about it, there's no point in trying to change your mind..."

I let him finish talking, looking him dead in the eyes throughout. Bone waited for a sign, a flicker, a movement, anything to give away my doubt and that his words hit the mark. I stared him down until he resigned to the fact I was no longer his partner. Whatever happened next, he would no longer be able to manipulate me, unless he resorted to threats.

"So what's been up with you?" he asked.

"Nothin' much. Mrs. Trent is not doing too well, so I'm keeping an eye on her."

"Who?"

"My neighbor, the old lady. I think I told you about her."

"Yeah, I guess. Why, she gon' croak?"

He had less than half a cup of coffee still left. As much as I wanted him gone, I also enjoyed watching the last of the person I would soon not have to do with anymore. In a sense, I was removing part of the weeds in the garden of my mind by cutting Bone off. He talked a bit about our last mission or something, I did not follow him as I continued to revel in the thought of estranging yet another old friend. At one point his phone rang. He talked fast and used his words sparingly, as they probably had a meaning only he and the other person on the phone knew.

"Duty calls," he got up after downing his coffee. "So, that's that?"

"Yes."

"OK. Talk to you soon then."

We shook hands in a cold, distant manner and Bone walked out. Another out and soon there would be no one left. Apart from me. I wondered if I would also get to see myself as an obstacle one day. If the same urge which drove me to alienate and block out everyone I knew somehow became pointed at myself, applying the same ruthlessness with which I treated those close to me, then it would all be over in no time. Since my garden had been almost completely emptied out, maybe that was the natural course of my path, the one that lay clear in front of me ever since adolescence. It had taken a long time for everything to come together and, during the previous year, it all came crashing down at an alarming speed. As the climax approached, it became obvious that I could not continue living like that. Seeing Bone leave, I sensed the conclusion to my story drawing near.

Like a gathering of dark clouds, or the unrelenting waves of an angry sea, a ceaseless stream of thoughts washed over me afterwards. Adrift in the ocean of time, I suddenly became obsessed with opening my eyes randomly and realizing I'd grown old in my own absence. I looked at my hand and imagined my own skin scorching into a livid husk and the flesh withering into a stringy corpse. Simultaneously, I could not get over myself yet utterly overlooked any sort of care or concern for my being and the outcome of my life.

Again, for three days I did not eat. I had food in the house, but the bread became stale and the two bananas on the counter turned black in the absence of someone to consume them. The greatest of problems returned, as I began to drastically lose my grip on reality.

The occasional grumbling interrupted my looping thoughts, sounding like the onset of an earthquake. I failed to trace the source of the distraction until I got up from the bed and noticed my stomach had stuck to my spine. Then I figured the grumbling must have resulted from my malnourished insides. I trailed to the kitchen and ate a piece of crusty bread, the part not yet touched by mold. Outside was dark and the house was silent. My inner universe felt the same way. In an instant, a sensation of falling in its immensity overwhelmed me, then a crushing feeling of the walls closing in on me took over. Losing my balance, I crouched down and waited for the whole thing to pass, which is when the creaking sound started ringing in my ears. To the steady rhythm of the creaks, the door to the storage room slowly opened by itself, with the darkness inside leaking out and blending into the shadow of the night. Not far enough away, I sensed it touching my skin, raising every hair on my body. During a brief silence, I shrunk into a ball of nervous terror, unable to think or act. A short thud came from the storage room, like a walking stick hitting the floor. Then the horrible cracks similar to stiff joints set into motion filled the apartment and drained my heart; I only got to see the glossy stubs of a plastic hand reaching out, because I sprung up, picked the car keys on the counter, and burst out of the apartment.

I slammed the door behind me as I fled, and did not distinguish anything around me other than the automatic light in the hallway and the suffocating silence of the outside world witnessing my nightmare.

Once outside, I ran around the building to my parking spot and jumped in the car. Shaking with fear and from the weakened state of my body, I turned the key too fast and the engine failed to start. Through the window, the corner of the building and the pavement stretching next to it, both yellow from the street lamps, had a cinematic air about them. Fiddling with the key, I wondered if the scene had actually taken place or if my mind played a trick on me. Immediately after, the mannequin showed up from behind the building in the same manner as predator stalking its prey. I got the car to start but the creature ran towards me with unnatural speed. Before I gained some distance from it, I heard the hellish sound of those plastic stubs tapping on the concrete while chasing me. I drove maniacally through the deserted town, from which all signs of life suddenly disappeared. Somehow, I had the composure to ask myself why the mannequin had never come to life when other people were around. However, when I looked in the rearview mirror and clearly saw it eating up the ground between us, dementedly throwing its limbs every which way to catch me, it was impossible to question the reality of the situation. All the while, the creaking continued and intensified, coming to resemble a myriad of overlapping saws, hacking and tearing away at my eardrums.

Eventually, I made it to the bridge, with the agitated stream of water under it like a trail of black blood. Having gone past the street lights, I came to rely on the mannequin's glimpses under the moonlight to be able to tell the distance between us. With its image appearing on and off the rearview mirror, the ghoulish creature seemed to have fallen behind. Nonetheless, I had to keep going for as long as possible.

Almost reaching the quarry, the sky cleared up entirely. A weird vibration animated the scene. It must have had to do with the clearing next to the quarry being the place where everything started. The glade opened up to my left as I drove by it, drawing me towards it. With no sight of the mannequin in my wake, I slowed down to get a better look at the area. Right before I drove past the clearing, the engine let out a nasty gurgle and died. I felt my heart about to burst as the shock left me dumbfounded, passing through me like an electric current or a hammer smashing every nerve in my body. I checked the rearview mirror: a white glimmer approached slowly from the distance.

Had it been a nightmare, I would have found myself paralyzed in the car until the mannequin reached me. Then I would have woken up the second it opened the door and laid its hand on me. Regardless, now I could move, and the only possible option was to get out and run away. And, although it seemed like the worst thing to do, I headed into the forest. The openness of the glade and the shadow of the trees behind it beckoned stronger than before. Leaving the car, the strange air filled my lungs and made my muscles quiver. The mannequin steadily closed in on me. And so, I took a deep breath and sprinted to the forest, diving straight into its obscurity.

Running through the trees, their crowns prevented the moonlight from seeping through. As my eyes were not adjusted to the complete darkness of the forest, the branches, twigs, and thorns scraped against my skin. I kept my hands in front of me to avoid hitting the trees. The woods swallowed me instantly, and the temporary burst of energy which led me there faded. Reaching nowhere, I stopped running and instead stumbled through the thicket, beaten down and tired. When my eyes finally adjusted, I tried to see whether the mannequin followed me or not. Besides the constant rustling of the leaves and the occasional snap, I did not see or hear anything suspicious. I sat down leaning against the tree closest to me and waited for the creaking in my ears to dwindle. A pleasant current of air grazed my face, hands, and hair, slowly carrying me away as I could feel myself dozing off somewhat, entering an on and off state similar to when I dreamt about Mrs. Trent in the asylum.

The trees and nature around me emanated a powerful energy, like a net, or water surrounding the bodies that swim in it. The fresh air from the trees, soft and velvety to touch, ran through my lungs sedating my body and mind. I wanted to stay there forever. The creaking in my ears left completely and I could hear the wind and my own steady breathing. As those sensations intensified and became all I knew and was, I started sinking into the earth while the bushes and the entire forest wrapped themselves around me, protecting me the way a womb nurtures its baby.

I continued to plummet until the sound of a voice stopped me. The clear, warm voice began talking to me and offering guidance to get back up again. It was my mother's voice.

"Don't allow yourself to fall asleep," she said. "This is not the end of the road and not the place where you should be. I have put all my love into you. Wake up, Chris. You have to keep going, you owe this to yourself. Take my hand and follow me."

Then I felt a soft touch on my hand. I stood up and walked forward, guided by my mother. Despite not turning my head to look at her, a strong white light glistened in the corner of my eye from the side and I knew it was her. She led me through an endless corridor, speaking to me along the way, although the farther we ventured, the more her words lost their meaning. When I realized we were going nowhere and just aimlessly wandering along the path, she spoke intelligibly again:

"This is not the right path. This is how you lived until now and it must stop. There, you just have to follow the light."

Not far from me, an opening emerged in the dark wall of the corridor. I listened to my mother and headed through. Then I found myself going down the asylum hallway in my dreams, bright and welcoming as always. She held my hand and walked me to the last room where Mrs. Trent waited. Unlike my dreams, she looked exactly the same as when we met: friendly, healthy, and most strikingly, happy. She smiled at me without saying anything.

"This is what you should be. What is good and right is in front of you. You only have to make the choice. Now is the time to do it, Chris."

I listened to her with my eyes closed. When she stopped speaking, I opened them again and instead of Mrs. Trent, I saw myself, glaring back with a plain expression. For the first time after years of frustration and contempt, I felt compassion for myself. Then, in profound silence, my projected self muttered through his lips:

"Help."

The crowns of the trees swished in the mellow wind, now a bit colder than before as the night went on. With great effort, I managed to detract my numb body from its support, the earth, and the trunk I'd been leaning against. In the calmness of the forest, there was no need for stealth or wariness as I sensed I was alone. With my eyes perfectly adapted to the obscurity, nature itself pointed me out, this time without scratches and cuts. I must have followed a slightly different path since I came across the log we used to prop up the mannequin, standing right in between the forest and the glade. The latter basked in the moonlight, creating a floaty, surreal atmosphere. Nothing around pointed at the ordeal which had taken place earlier, other than the abandoned car on the edge of the road.

The door had been open all throughout my visions in the woods. Inside the car I found nothing. With the key still in the lock, I turned it but the car refused to start. Then in a moment of inspiration, I lifted the hood and took the cap off the radiator. The liquid level was much below the line marking the optimal amount and luckily, I had a bottle of coolant in the trunk. I poured the substance into the engine and tried again to get the car going. It worked. The fact I knew what to do and had the answer to my problem at hand did not surprise me or make me happy, because I still felt being watched over by an invisible force.

As opposed to the harrowing scurry from my apartment to the forest, the drive back was slow and relaxed for the most part. I tried to enjoy the quiet stillness of the area and the fresh late air, although some tension lingered from the memory of the mannequin hunting me.

I crossed the bridge, approached the outskirts of the town, and leisurely moved along the streets. The buildings and the pavement were still heated by the summer sun. The temperature was pleasantly warmer than in the woods, and the street lamps flanking the road welcomed me under their cozy, intimate bolts of light. Disorderly and ridden with dust, a soothing familiarity settled in as the end of the trip drew near. However, the disturbing sight of a person stumbling and aimlessly ghosting through the street a bit farther than my apartment building put an end to my enjoyment. I parked the car and hesitantly walked towards the entrance to the flat, thinking the person might stop and interact with me. In the end, I had to approach and speak to the person myself when I realized it was, in fact, Mrs. Trent.

"What are you doing here?" I asked her bluntly.

"What?"

Her eyes were wide open with disorientation, and her arms gripped the buttons of her shirt as if to protect herself.

"Are you alright? Why are you out this late?" I asked.

"What do you want from me?"

I took a step towards her, but she made a grimace and brought her arms even closer to her body to defend against me. So, I kept my distance and tried talking to her softly instead.

"Do you know who I am?"

"No...do you want to rob me?" she stuttered.

"No, I just parked my car and wanted to go home. I live here, in this building. Where do you live?"

It seemed she tried to think about the answer, although I couldn't be sure what actually took place in her head. She only said, "I don't know."

"But didn't you get out of this building? I saw you coming out from here."

"Maybe. Why?"

"We are neighbors. I live in apartment 8, you live in number 7, opposite me. I'm Chris, we used to spend time together."

Mrs. Trent again took her time to process but shook her head in disbelief.

"I'm sorry, I don't know about any of that," she spoke.

"That's OK. Aren't you cold?"

"Am I cold...? A bit around my arms, yes. It must be late now."

"Yes, it is."

She wore her evening outfit and had walked out in her slippers. It might have been pleasant outside, but not for a weak, poorly dressed person, like me or Mrs. Trent.

"I was just about to go home and warm up over a cup of tea," I told her. "Would you care to join me?"

"I'm not sure if I should, I don't even know you after all..."

"I'm your neighbor, Chris. You are Mrs. Trent, you worked as a university professor in France and have a daughter, Samantha, who also lives there. We often have coffee together, and recently you bought me lemon ice cream."

"Did I?"

"Sure you did. And one of your favorite teas is chamomile. Let's just get in where it's warm, and I'll make you a cup."

I went to open the door and waved at her to come. Like a docile child, she listened and followed me upstairs to her apartment. As suspected, she hadn't locked her door before leaving, as the key was in fact still in the lock on the inside.

"Do you live here?" she asked me.

"No, you live here. I live right there next to you, see?"

"Oh."

I invited her to have a seat, gave her the blanket resting on the arm of the couch, and made her a cup of tea.

"It's much better here," she said while I cleaned some dishes. "I was actually quite cold outside."

"Yes, me too. It's good that we came in."

Or rather good that I found you, I thought to myself.

In the morning I made a call and had Mrs. Trent taken to a place where competent people could look after her until Samantha arrived in a few days and had her mother moved to the nursing home. She told Mrs. Trent, who at first vehemently rejected the idea, that it was a retirement community and that it would be merely a temporary thing until they came up with something better.

However, it was actually a nursing home, as we had no retirement communities in town, and taking Mrs. Trent to France would have been impossible since Samantha did not have the time to take care of her mother. I visited Mrs. Trent once soon after she moved, but since she did not recognize me, seeing her was painful for me rather than enjoyable for her, so it made little sense to keep doing it. I never visited Mrs. Trent again after that.

Chapter XII

As the first days of fall approached, not far after going to the nursing home to see my friend, Jane called to tell me she and Sophia would come over soon. Sophia had just returned from summer camp, where Jane sent her to make new friends besides the two she already had. If not for that, they would have flown over earlier as usual.

"Did it work out?" I asked.

"Surprisingly, yes" Jane answered. "She hated the first couple of days but I gave her an honest pep talk and apparently it had the desired effect."

"I'm guessing she didn't appreciate it at the moment."

"Definitely not, but what could she do? Anyway, we're only going to stay eight because school starts earlier this year around September 12."

"What did your parents say?"

"Well, they're disappointed, of course, but at the same time, they're glad for Sophia. Plus, they know it's only for this summer."

"That's how it starts..." I let out.

"What starts?"

"The older she gets, the less she'll stay when she visits them. After that, she'll start seeing them less and less. Distance creates more distance, it's inevitable."

"Well, hopefully not, Sophia loves her grandparents. That's a bit pessimistic to say, no?"

"Yeah, sorry. Maybe it won't be the case."

"You sound a bit down," she said concernedly, "is everything alright?"

"To be honest, it's not great, but I've been worse...way worse, so it's better now. A little lonely, that's all."

"Oh no," Jane said in a deeply sympathetic tone, "why? Aren't you hanging out with friends? What about your neighbor, why don't you spend some time with her?"

"She's in a nursing home now."

Jane held her breath for a moment, probably collecting her thoughts.

"The poor woman, that's horrible. Is she well taken care of there?"

"Yeah, she's in good hands."

"I'm sorry Chris, that is so sad to hear, I wish you told me earlier. It must have been depressing."

"It's sad, yes."

Maybe I should not have told Jane about it, but I'd shared nothing with her about any of my other problems. I'd used to be convinced that she genuinely cared about me, so keeping everything secret could be considered lying. I tried to protect her by doing it, or so I thought since she obviously could not help in any way, so learning about my issues in the recent past might have pointlessly burdened her. Or maybe I simply did not want to share my issues with anyone. I'd always had true and close friends who I used to talk to about everything. Yet, the trust, love, and humanity in my relationships deteriorated and eventually completely fell apart. Whether the morbidity deep within me led to that, or if it was rather a product of the growing chasm between me and the world. Since my mother, I hadn't said or heard the words "I love you" from anyone, which must have had a terrible effect in time. Anyhow, since my revelation in the forest, if it could be called that, I figured I could no longer hold it in me.

"At least Soph and I are coming to cheer you up, you can count on that," Jane spoke.

Hopefully so, but merely having them around for about a week might not help much this once. I'd been doing the bare minimum to take care of myself and cater to my needs. Other than occasionally feeding myself, I hadn't done much else. As proof of this, the greyness ran down my hand, stretching out from under the bandage and reaching halfway to my wrist. It spread onto my thumb and middle finger as well, with the last two the only ones that kept their sense of touch. I feared my whole hand might rot off at some point. However, I was too afraid to deal with it right then and there, so I took the tape and wrapped some new layers over the affected part.

For the rest of the day, I cleaned the apartment in an attempt to undo the harm and neglect it had seen. Hearing Jane's voice put me in a frantic state which led to the thorough cleansing of my home, apart from the storage room which remained locked. I threw away the little old and rotten food still laying around, took out the trash, and even got rid of the two dead peaches. At some point, I also remembered the envelope from Bone, which had been laying on the counter in plain sight. I took it and put it away in a drawer, although I initially wanted to throw it away. Throughout the process, it dawned on me how I'd never been able to find meaning in life, and how that continuous struggle brought on the deep sense of pressure embedded in me, which gradually translated into a physical sensation of weight in my chest. As the depression worsened, it must have degenerated into something more grievous, which was what I began to experience when the mannequin entered my life. With the spiritual need left unanswered for so long, mental illness came in as a consequence of the increasing urgency to find purpose. Depression pointed that out, but the onset of mental illness revealed the dire consequences of failing to do so. Thinking about that, it finally became clear that the episode in the forest, the vision of my mother guiding me through the darkness, was not some sort of intervention or a fortunate epiphany. It was, in truth, the final warning that I had to fix the broken, worthless life I lived.

Coincidence had it that Ritchie called me a couple hours later after talking to Jane. I let the phone ring and pressed the side button to put it on silent. When a few minutes passed, I told him to text me if he wanted to talk, since I did not want to deal with him directly. He replied immediately, asking me to go over to his house and clarify our situation. I told him we had nothing to clarify, but Ritchie pleaded with me to hear him out. Angered by his stubborn refusal to accept that I'd ended our friendship, I felt the sudden impulse to meet him, even though I knew nothing good would come out of it. In a mean, somewhat childish manner, I wanted to go over and have him beg for my friendship only so I could show Ritchie how little I cared for him. In other words, I wanted to take out my resentment on him. I told him I would go by the next day at noon.

The chestnuts' leaves had scorched in the arid heat of the sun. The dry and barren soil stretched exhausted on both sides of the pathway between the fence and the house. It must have been a particularly hot summer, although, trapped in my own head, I failed to register that. Replacing the irritation that animated my steps towards Ritchie's house, the sight of it evoked a strange, almost apathetic sadness. It was weird not to think with some sort of endearment of that place. Even in the stagnant and then irksome stages of our friendship, whenever I went to Ritchie's house it felt like the unpleasantness was merely a temporary thing, as the underlying basis of fondness would prevail again in the future. In retrospect, however, when the image of something does not match the reality of the situation is what makes a relationship toxic. As the irritation faded and I walked through the chestnuts onto the porch, I mourned my friendship with Ritchie.

Knocking on the door, he answered unusually fast. Probably not many people knocked on his door lately. I read on his face the mixture of gladness and cautiousness at seeing me again. I also read in his shakiness the fact that he'd drunk, likely out of necessity rather than anything else.

"Come in," he said, then added reticently "thank you for dropping by."

I walked in. He told me to keep my shoes on and invited me to have a seat. The left side of the couch used to be my spot, but now I sat in the armchair.

"Can I offer you anything?" Ritchie asked standing up. "Coffee, beer?"

"Just water."

He returned with two glasses of water and an ashtray. When he lit a cigarette, he offered me one too, which I refused.

"What have you been up to?" Ritchie spoke.

"Been doing my bit, nothing much other than that. You?"

He nodded in reply, looking for words, for anything to say to me. Without directly admitting it, he'd been doing as poorly as ever also. We both must have dealt with the pressure of time passing with nothing to show in return. Besides the alcohol, that too contributed to his aging overnight.

"I've been thinking about the argument we had, you know, a while ago. It doesn't make sense to me that such a petty thing stood in our way this long. We should just get over it and put it to bed. What do you say?"

I tried to remember precisely what had gone on during the fight, but I only remembered that he shoved me out of the house. Then I figured he must have said something about me and Jane, something I always suspected him to hold against me, even though he surely did not believe I slept with her. He created that out of resentment about the fact my relationship with his ex-wife and daughter was better than his.

"It is petty. But you're the same person who said those things, and I'm certain you would do it again if you got the chance. I'm done with that."

Those ice-cold words flew out of me with a slapping indifference towards Ritchie, whose face instantly dropped. I'd never been confrontational with him, apart from the fight.

"What? Hold on, I don't know where you're getting this from. Did I ever say anything like that to you?"

"Not so directly, but you were always bothered about how well I get along with Jane and Sophia. Even the faces you make, it's not hard to imagine what you're thinking. Honestly, for how good a friend I've been to you, I don't deserve that."

It took him a bit to let it sink in. However, his temper started to flare up as usual when things weren't going his way. He leaned forward before speaking to me:

"Then it's also not hard to understand why I have those thoughts in my head when you've always stuck around her, even after she got with me. You can't seriously tell me you weren't waiting for things to go wrong with us so you could jump in and get a second chance."

I stared him down, unwilling to defend myself for something I wasn't guilty of, especially in front of him.

"I believe you're envious of me," Ritchie resumed. "Don't imagine I liked seeing you hung up like that. I can't remember if you've ever had a serious relationship after that, so I understand what you felt for her. But it's not like I did anything to you. I just acted according to how I felt and unfortunately things didn't work out. It's how it was meant to be."

"You're wrong. I've never envied you because I knew it would only bring me sorrow and ruin my friendship with both of you. I'm only sorry for Jane for having to raise Sophia by herself when someone like her deserves so much better. And I resent you for that, as well as having Sophia grow up without a father."

Ritchie faced those words with an unusual solemnity for him. Maybe, as a change, he respected the honesty behind what I said rather than not taking it seriously. He looked down and seemed deep in thought for a while.

"I regret that myself, about not being there for Sophia, and I would change that in a heartbeat if it was that easy. But you're still not the person to criticize me for it."

We locked eyes throughout the exchange, then looked away from each other to leave room for thoughts to take place. I reached for the glass and when I finished drinking and put it back, I took a cigarette from the pack on the table and lit it up. Ritchie did the same. We smoked in silence, then he said:

"I messed up a lot, but having this kind of relationship with my daughter is the only thing I wish I could go back in time for. All else, I can live with."

Silence again. Tiny tapping sounds came from the window, but I couldn't tell what caused them because the blinds were shut. They quickly intensified, and when I heard the deep grumble in the distance, I recognized the early autumn rain. It fell down at a mellow pace and lasted little, but when I soon walked out the sky was still clouded.

"What's the worst thing you ever did?" Ritchie spoke suddenly.

I figured from the manner he said it that he wanted to play the mutual confession game, then somehow make the point of us being rather similar in the end, or how no one is perfect and that we should resolve our differences and be friends. The tiny bit of compassion I began having for him melted away, and I answered bluntly:

"I don't know. Anyway, that's how I feel and it's not gonna change."

"You sure?"

"Yeah. I think both of us should head different ways at this point."

"Maybe you're right. OK," he exhaled, "so be it."

I finished my water and stood up. Ritchie got up too, looked into my eyes, and shook my hand with nothing but dignity. Without speaking to each other, I went out and he closed the door behind me. The chestnuts' bark darkened under the rain, and the soil's color turned into a mineral grey.

Fall was my favorite season. In my heart, I'd lived in a perpetual autumn, aesthetically and spiritually. Marked by a certain ripeness of thought and sentiment, the sweet spot right between the treacherous enthusiasm of youth, like summer, or the slowing down and fadedness of winter. Never fully happy, nor hopeless to the point of suicide, life, at best, was of a sublime bittersweet, like the sound of a violin or, at its worst, exasperatingly bland. In perfect synchronicity with nature, my whole being reached the sweet spot once more, the musical clarity which allowed me to cut off the last weeds in my garden, and have left the only thing which truly mattered to me.

The thought of Jane and Sophia arriving made a greater impact on me than before. I sensed something had to happen, or rather the need to make something happen myself. Things have a mysterious way of letting you know when they're about to take place, something which makes you desire that thing with all your heart, and by doing so you believe that you're ultimately ready for it to happen. With Jane's image in my head, I'd never felt anything so intensely before. Now more than ever, I wanted to be happy.

I did not know precisely how I should proceed, but I decided to let the flow of things guide me. The second day since their plane touched down, as always, she called me to hang out.

"It's so much more bearable here than it is in Italy right now," she said referring to the heat. "And I love this time of year too, it's just perfect for going out. What do you wanna do?"

"Hmm," I said. We could go for coffee somewhere as usual, or they would come over to mine and we'd hang out on the balcony. However, looking at the two peach trees, they were beginning to outgrow their pots, so I would have to replant them in the coming weeks. It pained me to think I'd have to prune them one day. They should be left alone to follow their course and grow naturally as much as possible, without human intervention.

"I have an idea," I told Jane. "How about we go out for a snack by the old quarry? There's a nice spot close to the forest, and I have a couple of trees I thought of planting there."

"I'd love that, definitely. Soph, wanna go plant Chris' trees?"

"YES!" she shouted in the background.

"Then we have a plan," Jane said. "When should we go?"

"Around five-thirty would be best. There'll still be a few hours of sun but it won't be too hot...for me."

"Yeah, I wanted to say that," she chuckled. "Then I'll fix us a little picnic basket, and you can get the shovels I suppose. Let me know when you're coming over to pick us up."

Maybe my situation truly completed a full circle, since I got to await with pleasure the act of digging a hole. I still had the shovel from the last mission in my trunk, so I only needed a container with water for the trees once they were planted. And that was that. I could simply relax and enjoy myself while the hours passed until meeting Jane and Sophia. Which I did.

They were waiting for me in front of the building where Jane's parents lived. Jane wore a marine blue dress which went down to her knees and some round sunglasses. She had her hair tied in a ponytail, which I thoughted suited her perfectly. Sophia, on the other hand, wore outside clothes, comfortable and good for playing around in nature. She also had a sailor hat on, which Jane must have insisted on. Sophia sat down on the stairs, while Jane stood up with a backpack and a large yellow shopping bag by her side. I stopped the car in front of them, although Sophia jumped up when she first saw it, while Jane greeted me with her beautiful smile. I hugged Soph, picking her up and spinning her in the air as she liked, then held Jane in my arms long and tight, forcing myself to let go of her eventually.

"Are those the trees?!" Soph asked when she opened the back door.

"Yes, they're peaches. If we plant them right, we can grow our own fruit in a couple of years."

"They're so thin though."

"Yeah, but they're young. They don't mind the cold, so they're going to be more than happy with their new place."

"Was it these two that I saw last time?" Jane asked.

"These and two others, but those didn't make it, unfortunately."

"Aha. These are beautiful by the way, two out of four is a good ratio considering they're not cultivars. Or are they?"

"No, they came from the peaches I have at the store. It can't get more homegrown than this."

Sophia sat in the back with her arm across one of the pots. I took the bag and the backpack and put them in the trunk, next to the shovel and the water canister.

"What's in here?" I asked Jane about the bag.

"A light potato salad, a few strawberries my parents bought, some apple juice for Soph, and coffee for us."

"Great. Ah, that bucket, I don't think we had a trip where you didn't bring that with us." Jane had a picnic set made of one orange bucket containing small plastic plates and cups, and one larger plate as a lid. They were all the same color – orange, and Jane must have had them for at least fifteen years.

"Of course," she said. "I've grown really attached to it. I always take it when we go to the beach in Bari."

We went and sat in the car. I checked the rearview mirror before driving away and spotted Soph examining the trees. Jane put up her sunglasses and gazed at the surroundings as we drove by. A wonderful sensation began to take shape. I strongly felt the presence of both Jane and Sophia with me in the car, how well we gelled as a unit, and the harmony between us. It was as if our togetherness created a shield against the world and everything sad, painful, or uncertain in it. Now that I got to live such a moment again, as well as being grateful for it, I desperately wished it could last forever. The sublimity of the love between us created a window to eternity, in front of which my being disintegrated at the thought of being dragged down by the weight of every passing second and sunken into a place without Jane and Sophia, the ordinary, loveless, fleeting world. With those images lurking in the back of my mind, I tried to chase them away and focus on the present. It worked until Sophia asked suddenly:

"Chris, what happened to your hand?"

Jane also turned to look at me, having not paid attention to the bandage before.

"I burned the back of my hand on the stove, so I put some cream on it and patched it up to heal properly."

"Does it hurt?"

"It's quite numb actually. It only hurt at first."

"Can I dig the hole?" she went on.

"For the trees?"

"Yeah."

"If you're able to, sure."

"Of course I'm able."

"Have you dug a hole before?"

"Yes."

"Not in the ground you haven't," Jane intervened.

"Same thing," Sophia argued.

"The shovel may be a bit too big for you," I said.

"I can handle it, you'll see."

"Alright then. I'm not gonna stand in your way."

We arrived at the clearing in front of the forest. I parked on the side of the road and then picked up the water canister and one pot. Jane took the backpack and the yellow shopping bag, while Soph wanted to carry the other tree.

"Leave it here, I'll get it. You can take the shovel and find us a nice spot for the trees."

She took the shovel, slightly too thick for her hands and roughly as tall as her, and ran towards the field.

"Can't remember when I last came here," Jane spoke. "Which is crazy, because it's such a nice place and it's so close to my parents' house."

"I could come more often myself, but it's not as much fun to do it alone."

We walked down onto the field. Jane placed down the bag and took off the backpack then laid a blanket on the grass while I brought the peach tree to where Sophia had stuck the shovel in the ground.

"Is this good?" she asked.

"Perfect. Just so that they'll be close to the others, but also stick out a bit so we can recognize them once they've grown."

She revealed her satisfaction with a grin.

"Should I start digging?" she asked.

"Yeah, let's get it done."

I went to grab the other tree while she tried her hand at shoveling. When I returned, I showed her that she could press the shovel with her foot to push it down more easily.

"We can do one each," I told her.

"Can I do both myself?" she said.

"If you want."

I let her dig both holes while I went over to the blanket and sat next to Jane. The light of the evening sun bounced off her hair and her beautiful tanned legs. Without a word, she took out two cups from the bucket and poured us coffee out of the thermos.

"She asked to do it herself?" Jane pointed at Sophia.

"Yeah. Seems like she's having fun."

"She is. We're gonna have to visit the trees every time we come back from Italy now, I already know it."

We both took a drink. The coffee was strong but good, almost as intense as an espresso.

"What have you been up to Chris? How's life?"

"What can I say, I try to stay afloat. Some days are better than others I suppose."

"I've been thinking about that phone call we had a while ago. Is there anything I can help out with? You know I'm here for you if you need something, anything..."

She touched my forearm as she said that. We made eye contact, and the unbounded affection and care I saw in her nearly brought down all my walls of defense. I gazed at her long enough for my heart to warm up from the love of another human being towards me, and looked away at the last moment, or else I would have broken down into tears. However, Jane must have picked up on it because she moved closer and put her arms around me, which is when I could not hold it in anymore. I put my head down and wept. As she comforted me, the feeling of her hand moving from the back of my head down to my neck sent shivers down my spine. What I felt was too much to comprehend, it was simply overwhelming. Jane held me in silence, and when the tears stopped, I could hear the shovel hitting the ground in the distance. Luckily, Jane's hug muffled the little noise I might have made, thus

Sophia didn't realize what happened. Eventually, I lifted my head from Jane's embrace.

"Thank you," I said. She squeezed my hand and said nothing because nothing needed to be said. I wiped my face and we both stretched out quietly under the now orange sun for a couple of minutes, until Sophia called out that she finished digging the second hole.

"You got a knife?" I asked Jane.

"Yeah. Here it is," she said taking it out of the bucket and handing it to me.

The holes were pretty wide. I only took out a couple of extra shovels of dirt to make them deeper. Then I tipped over the pots and worked the knife around the inner edge between the plastic and the dirt while rolling the containers sideways. Once I did that enough, I poured out the contents of the pots and what came out was a round solid mass of roots and soil. Together with Sophia, we separated the dirt from the roots and untangled them, and placed the first tree into its new home. Meanwhile, Jane watched from the side, taking the occasional photo to have as a memory. Sophia then filled up the hole with dirt and I only patted it down a bit in the end, before repeating the process with the other tree as well. To finish it off, I brought the big container over and watered the peaches so the roots would fixate quicker. As we admired our work, Jane wanted to take a photo of us between the trees, which were about three meters apart from one another. Then she set up a timer and placed her phone on the bucket while we all took a photo together, like a family.

Afterwards, we sat on the blanket and ate the salad. Being near the forest, it got cold faster than on the heated concrete of the town. The light gradually grew dimmer until a heavy blue soaked the sky, so Jane called Sophia, who had gone to explore the surroundings, and we steadily packed and got ready to leave. Ever since Jane held me in her arms earlier and touched me with such rare tenderness, I kept buzzing inside as my body remembered the heat of her body. And the two peaches which survived now became part of the forest, that mystical place which, for better or worse, played such an important part in my life. From higher up on the road and looking down at the clearing, they stood out visibly to my eyes, although mainly because I knew they were mine. In a way, having them planted there signified the end of a cycle, a dark and terrible one. And while those thoughts took place, I could not ignore the overpowering attraction I started feeling towards Jane again after all those years. Maybe everything happened as it did, and in that precise order, for a reason. And maybe since those emotions returned exactly when I managed to leave my problems behind, it might have been the universe's way of telling me that Jane was, at long last, that reason.

Chapter XIII

The following two days I didn't see them. Jane and Sophia were busy spending time with family and other friends, so I was left to ponder what I should do next. For two nights I barely slept, waking up early, even before the sun made its way up. Worried about the limited opportunities left to see them till their flight back to Italy, I asked Jane to see me. She said Sophia would go to see Ritchie, although we could hang out just the two of us. And for the second consecutive morning, I woke up and went out on the balcony, unable to continue sleeping.

The lingering shadow of the past lifted off my soul. Incredibly, and perhaps without precedent, I faced an open future ahead of me. Between getting home after planting the trees and seeing Jane in private, my mind took off, contemplating every possible scenario for what could happen. However, unlike back when the mannequin dominated my existence, and I used to drown under the flow of thoughts when thinking about Jane I did so animated by the fresh breath of life and with the impulse to love and progress. I did not plan precisely what to do, but I knew I had to make my feelings clear to her.

As that vital inspiration spurred me to find a solution, the rising sun brought along some movement on my street, with the entire town lying dormant until then. Down the street, from around the corner and heading towards the garbage bins, the homeless man with his three-legged dog. Yet on this occasion, they were not alone, because walking besides the old man was a little girl, most likely his granddaughter.

She and the dog waited while the man completed the scavenging routine. The little girl held the man's stick while he did so, waving it around like a sword and pointing it at the dog. Despite their situation, the girl and the man both had a certain leisure or even joy about them. They clearly relished each other's company and blocked out everything else it seemed. I couldn't see the man's arms but judging by his movement he found something useful and put it in his bag. Then he glanced at the side of the bin, where a blue plastic bag hung. The man searched it and found a scarf and other smaller things, perhaps some underwear or socks. He examined the scarf and smelled it; it must have been clean since it was placed next to the bin rather than in it. He turned around, bent down, and wrapped it around the girl's neck. The first days of September had come, so the mornings were already quite cold. Both the man and the little girl were dressed in thick clothes; she propped the stick against the bin and touched the material of the scarf with both hands, studying the patterns on it. The man quickly checked the other bin and then put the bag over his shoulder, with the girl handing him the stick and taking his hand. They behaved so gently with one another, in a manner only possible between grandparents and their grandchildren. I could only think back to my grandfather and remember when I used to feel his love and protection all around me as a child, and also remember when I used to have a family. The old man and the girl definitely did not have much, but they had each other and, more importantly, they had love.

A love expressed negatively; that is what I had for Jane. That is what she allowed me to have, or what I dared not surpass. I missed her when she was not around, and when we were finally together, I could not get close enough to her. I yearned for her and she attracted me like the shining light of a faraway star. She welcomed me, but from a distance; Jane possessed a warm remoteness, or attractive neutrality, which I imagined would raise a barrier between us before I got too close, or as much as I wanted and needed. You can never get close enough to someone like Jane. Maybe I just overextended her rejection when she chose Ritchie over me. The fact now I had no other option than to go for it gave me courage, because it meant it was the right thing to do.

I met Jane at eleven o'clock at noon, in between the morning chills and the remnants of the summer heat in the evening. We went for a walk and headed towards the bridge, picking up coffee on the go.

"My parents asked if I find it alright for Sophia to be spending time alone with Ritchie," she told me. "Of course, they couldn't possibly have a good image of him after how we separated."

"I don't think that would ever be a cause for concern. We don't talk anymore, but I know he loves Sophia. She's pretty much all he has left."

"Yeah, that's what I told them. But I get their worries, I barely keep in touch with him these days and saw him maybe six or seven times at most for the past five years."

"What does Soph make of it?"

"That her parents don't talk to one another?"

"No, that you guys split up and she gets to see him once a year."

"Well, she's aware he's having some problems and understands he's not exactly capable of raising a child as it is. But she realizes it has nothing to with her, or with Ritchie not loving her."

"She seems to cope well with it," I said.

"Yeah, she just takes it as it is, fortunately."

We went past the store where Mrs. Trent forgot her groceries once, where we stopped to buy a bottle of water. Then without entering the park, we walked parallel to the wide alley in the middle of it. The alley and the trees by its sides formed the entire park, actually. Moving on, the buildings dispersed as we neared the bridge. I nudged Jane towards a bench under a tree, the last resting spot before leaving the center of town and heading into the outskirts.

"There's a certain charm about this time of year. I can't point out what exactly makes it like this," Jane said, "it's rather a mix of things. There's this warm air which you can feel on your skin, but not hot to the point where it's uncomfortable. There's also this growing difference between night and day, that you have to take into account when going out. And even the colors are starting to change, see?" she pointed at the slightly crispy leaves above us. "Such a distinctive period this, like a strange mix of change and stillness. Wasn't fall your favorite season by the way?"

"Yes, it is."

"Yeah, I thought you mentioned it. It'd also be my favorite one if it was entirely like this. But there's also rain and dullness later on, and I'm not such a fan of that."

"I like that as well. It's the only period I go for walks willingly."

A moment passed when a car drove by us, stirring behind it the prematurely fallen leaves.

"You should come visit us in Italy then," Jane added. "There's a rainy season there like nowhere else if you're interested. Most of winter is like that."

"I'll seriously consider it. I thought about visiting you there sometime. I don't know why I haven't already, maybe because I'm used to having you come home instead."

"Me too, actually. I still think about here as home. Soph too."

"Now that you mention it, do you plan on staying there for good? Maybe until Sophia finishes her education?"

"I've tried to think of something, but I can't imagine the future that far ahead. I just can't do it for some reason, so I'm taking it one year at a time for now."

"Aha, I can relate to that."

"What about you? What do you want your future to hold?"

"What I want from my future..."

She looked at me waiting for a reply. I could sense her anticipation, how she really wanted to know and how her curiosity overthrew her usual principle of letting people be, having them open the subject if they wanted to. Not that asking a friend about general future plans lacked discretion or violated anyone's privacy, yet even from Jane's perspective, in my case it felt different.

"Look, I don't mean to be nosy, but I could tell by that moment the other day that something is wrong, or that you're not doing well, which was kind of a wake-up call for me."

"How so?" I asked, with nervous suspense starting to build up in me.

"I realized we haven't been together in so long; as in properly together. Like our relationship has been put on hold indefinitely, living so far from one another and both of us busy with our separate lives. And whenever we meet, we're not exactly present I feel, we're more just 'there'. And for that reason, I've become out of touch with what you must have been through, which really bothers me."

I tried not to choke up and retain composure since that conversation had been overdue between us. At the same time, I wanted to touch Jane and have her close to me, wrap ourselves around each other and kiss. I'd been longing for that kiss for over ten years, and now I wanted to open up my ribcage and pull her inside my chest, and finally be together.

"I've noticed that as well," I struggled to contain myself, "but I tried not to mention it because I figured we could do nothing about it."

"I don't know..." she spoke.

I looked at her possessed by the thought of kissing her, by the softness of her lips and the warmth of her embrace, passion and desire burned up in me and I could no longer resist, although the last morsel of awareness I still had prevented me from touching her. Instead, I said:

"Jane...I love you."

She looked at me. The split second she understood how I meant it, a slight change in her facial expression caused the entire world to disintegrate inside my head since I realized she did not feel the same for me. Instantly, I withered inside, with the shred of spirit left intact preventing me from collapsing in front of her.

"Chris..."

I dreaded hearing the rest of it, although the worst had just happened.

"You know I love you and my affection for you is endless. Please believe how awful it is for me to be that one person who ends up hurting you, I only ever wanted the best for you, and I truly wish this could be mutual, you're an extraordinary human being and..."

All else flew by me, and through me. Even the breeze passed through me, as I became hollower than the air itself. I watched Jane talk without hearing her, and felt how the distance between us increased at light speed until I died and she became a memory of myself and the life I'd left behind. I fell and fell until darkness came over me, and darkness what the last thing I knew.

It was suddenly tight, dark, and uncomfortable when a terrible claustrophobic sensation came upon me. The pressure coming from outside caused it, submerged deep in that water, pitch black because of the night. The submarine happened to be close to the middle of the gulf, and I must have been traversing it without any problems so far since uneasiness only struck me about halfway through. I stopped, aware that turning back would be impossible for some unknown reason, yet something prevented me from making it to the other shore. A faint vibration passed through the metal floor, and the submarine went up and down slightly as if riding a wave. The discomfort then turned into angst, when my sight switched to a bird's eye view of the water, framed between the two shores. The dock lay closer to me than I initially thought, with a few scattered lights revealing the buildings behind. I recognized my town, although the shapes and textures were much different than in reality, and also there were no other waters besides the river. I got the hunch that what I experienced did not actually take place in reality, although it didn't occur to me that it was in fact a dream. Maybe because I had no time to realize it since from my view from above I observed a large wave spread across the water, while simultaneously being in the submarine when it swayed under it. Without seeing it, I sensed the presence of the thing inhabiting the water, and an enormous fear rattled me. The creature prowled the water while I remained stuck in the submarine, waiting for something to happen.

Then abruptly, as if the overload of terror brought on the next scene in the dream, I found myself in my old college room, located close to the dock I had to reach. Lying in bed, I sat up and looked out the window to see the inky water mirroring the sky. I watched on, struggling to apprehend the size of the gulf and the actual distances between things, like between the room and the dock, or the water and the sky. Perhaps everything morphed when I didn't look, which actually made sense. From the corner of my eye, I spotted a pale light up in the sky, now right above me, biting into the ceiling. The light respawned here and there repeatedly until more lights appeared altogether and created a dancing circle, which gradually became a disk floating above me. The thing went away when I heard a distant splash and quickly glanced at the water to see a massive shape swirling just above the surface and then submerging again. Petrified, I waited in my room as nothing happened the following moments, suddenly for the monster to wriggle again and a myriad of disks raging over the town and the water. The sky itself started palpitating epileptically, switching between red and yellow in an apocalyptic show of colors. The world was coming to its end, raucous, blinding, and hellish. I felt it crumbling, with myself along it. Then completely naturally, I stood up, embracing the last moments of existence, and spoke out loud: "I am here, and it is my time to become."

I lied with my eyes closed, focusing on each breath until I calmed down. Peeking through my eyelids, the shadows moved rhythmically as the branches waltzed in the moonshine. Slowly, turning on my left side to see the window of my bedroom, the chair and lamp sat in their same old spots. I inhaled deeply and with ease, after exiting the submarine in my nightmare. I gazed out the window for a short while and then tried to go back to sleep, but a luminous shard highlighted a portion of the wall in the hallway where usually the moonlight did not reach. It must have been my phone so I went to check, hoping in the back of my mind that Jane had reached out. Squinting at the bright screen, it was a message on Ritchie. I tapped twice to open it and saw one of the photos from the other day when Jane, Sophia, and I went planting. Underneath, it wrote "Sweet pic. You'd make a nice family together. I guess she doesn't know what a hypocrite you are."

The anger set off gripping my heart and quickly swelled up to the point of bursting out of my chest. Then it traveled up and my forehead became heavy as led while I panted uncontrollably, grinding my teeth. To be hit where it hurt the most, after all that suffering, by the pettiest of people and with such wickedness...My head whirled, and the blood in my veins turned into poison as I lost control and started wailing out of frustration. It only stopped when the most unusual dizziness, nullifying and morbid, wiped me out completely.

Vegetating in a strange dormancy, I could not move or think. The only things which happened were the sounds of a door slowly opening, followed by footsteps and then another door closing. I remained half-conscious throughout. The image of the well in my grandfather's garage steadily took shape. While it did, I knew I was sinking in that water. My air slowly ran out, with every second carrying the weight of impending fatality. The water remained painfully still until one bubble rose from its depths and sat on the surface. I held my breath and fought for life, with my lungs about to collapse. Then, at the last second, the bubble popped.

The diffuse light of the early morning's blue hours sneaked into the room. A slumbering heaviness burdened my body, and my eyes were dry and tired. No surprise that I rested so poorly. My back ached and my limbs were numb with fatigue. Also, my fingers felt sticky for some reason. I clenched my left fist and worried that I'd lose tactility in that hand as well, yet the sensation persisted. Not without difficulty, I opened my eyes which could not yet see clearly, but the light and the creases accentuated some areas of the duvet over the rest. I moved my legs, but the spots remained darker than the color of the blanket. Then I propped my head up and removed my hand from under the duvet to grab it when the blood struck me. Both my hands were painted in dark, tacky blood, with marks trailing over the blanket and through to the hallway.

Full of dread, I followed the traces which led to the storage room. A large stain leaked out from inside, and I feared what I would find in there. Leaving the lights off, I cracked the door slightly and distinguished the mannequin's outline in the dark. It seemed to be in the same position I'd left it in. However, a puddle of blood lay at its base, with a couple of legs outstretched over and through it. Terrified, I reached out for the switch, although for a split second I imagined the mannequin grinning at me with unholy satisfaction. I turned the light on and slowly leaned forwards, glancing around the corner to see Ritchie's body slumped to the side with a burgundy stream running down his shirt. Now dried out, it had poured out from the gunshot in his head, right above the eyebrow. Equally desperate and confused, I stepped back, unable to process the situation. On the coffee table close to me, a gun. The same one Bone gave me at the hall when we were attacked. I remembered throwing it into the glovebox of the car, forgetting about it completely afterwards. Trying to piece together those notions, I reached into my pockets and found the car key, which I usually never carried with me. Leaning on the counter and holding my head, I noticed the cellphone there and instantly recalled Ritchie's message and how everything cut off abruptly after reading it. That mitigated the shock of seeing him dead in my storage room. However, it left me in a deeply alienating and uncomfortable situation, since I could easily black out at any moment. Frighteningly, the point had come when I could no longer trust myself.

At the risk of losing control again, I rushed over to the car while able to and grabbed the trash bags in the trunk, always at the ready. Remarkably, there were no traces of blood on the stairs in my building, despite my apartment being a mess. The cold bit into my flesh, countering the fear, the weakness in my heart, and nausea in my stomach, although it added to the tiredness. All I wanted was to sink into a soft mattress and pull a warm cover over my head, somewhere safe and quiet, away from everything. While wrapping Ritchie up and scrubbing the floor, both difficult tasks in my condition, all I could really think of was the mannequin. I put it away before getting to work because I could not stand being near it or having it in my field of vision. Even with a wall between us, now out in the open and no longer locked up, I sensed it glaring at me or at least focusing its energy on me. Wiping Ritchie's blood off and pulling down trash bags over his gunshot gaping forehead should have at least distracted me from thinking about the mannequin. But it didn't.

With the room relatively cleared and with my former friend's body swathed in multiple layers of plastic, the only thing which made sense next was to call Bone and ask for help. I did not know how I'd carried Ritchie by myself unless I'd somehow made him come over and then killed him. I knew, however, that I could not move the body alone, then dig up a hole and stand in the forest alone at night. Calling Bone would surely lead to other complications, but I did not care. My only concern was getting rid of the kill as soon as possible. So, I picked up the phone and made the call.

"Hey," Bone spoke, perhaps surprised, indifferent, or both.

"I need your help."

"Oh yeah?"

"Yeah. Cleaning."

Hearing that caught him off guard. Not immediately after, but he asked in a serious tone:

"What the hell? Where?"

"Mine."

"Jesus...OK. I'll be there later. I'm currently busy, and we can't do it now anyway."

I had to wait until nightfall to move the body. That meant that the entire day I had to stand by the corpse as well as the mannequin, awakened by the murder and rejuvenated by the blood. Obviously, I could not afford to leave in that unstable frame of mind. Besides, I had no place to seek refuge either. So, I waited.

The hours passed. The daytime brightness gracefully bowed to the expanding shadow. The arbitrary recollection of Mrs. Trent's decline, which replayed in my head while waiting for Bone, unveiled with fresh clarity the disregard and even contempt I'd begun to foster against my friend. Re-examining the past, I fell deeper into contemplation and grew desensitized to the mannequin's aura. Further on, a pattern emerged as I began to understand how my detachment from the world had been a long, continuous process and how, to a large degree, I'd never been a normal, functional person. Crouched up on the couch until then, I loosened up and let go of the tension built up from earlier, lying down and closing my eyes to think. Doing so, I completely blocked out the mannequin and the body resting on the floor so close to me.

Even before I lost my mother, trying to retain some semblance of interest and engagement with the outside struck me as hopelessly shallow. Then, since my mother's passing, the constant sensation of falling out of the world and into myself increased until it became a crushing norm. And perhaps reaching that point, to protect itself, my mind created a state of perplexity to keep ruin at bay. In lack of anything substantial, my relation to the world consisted of frail stability, maintained by a defective, sterile routine. It resisted valiantly until a few unfortunate events dismantled my defense and left me utterly exposed.

It makes sense that people are supposed to fade into the world, blend in and become part of it.

Death has the purpose of finalizing the process and making us become one with the world, integrating us into its universal soul. Whereas I've never been part of this, because I observed it too lucidly and, fatally, too early. With the sun going down under the rooftops behind my window, I understood I couldn't lose my mind, simply because there was nothing there to be lost. And while watching the mannequin's energy dissipate and seeing it become a lifeless piece of plastic once more, I understood that it had represented my actual last resort. All that time, I'd projected my subconscious onto it, animating it and creating that horrible distraction to hide my own emptiness and fundamental lack of belonging. I floated because that's what I was, thus madness could only be normal to me. Featureless, strange, and empty, I'd had no other enemy but myself the entire time.

The dawn crept up on us quickly when I came back to my senses. I'd made my mind up, and planned not to come back home, whatever happened that night. I simply could not do it, unable to start over there nor continue living that way. I expected Bone to arrive at any moment and decided to take care of something while I still had time. I crouched over the mannequin and looked at it, waiting to see if it made me feel anything. The bruised purple I'd once witnessed spread under my eyes and all over the mannequin's torso had disappeared. The wounds no longer bled and the heartbeat ceased forever. The mannequin had lost its power over me. I stood above a sad, cut-up piece of plastic and nothing more. Rather tired, I picked it up and went to throw it in the trash bin outside. However, the homeless man with the little girl came to mind. I would probably never see them again, and I still hadn't left them anything. I placed the mannequin outside in front of the door came back and opened the drawer with Bone's unopened envelope. I found a pen and wrote on it with capital letters "FOR YOU AND YOUR FAMILY," then put it in a plastic bag together with some fruit and old sweets I had in the house. Next, I went outside to the bin, dumped the mannequin, and hung the bag with the envelope by the side of the trash. The bin was relatively empty, so the garbage workers would not come before the old man had the chance to find the envelope. Once back in the house I drank a glass of water, put the gun under my belt, and waited for Bone to come. The body lay in the middle of the room, ready to be taken away. I said to Ritchie "I don't know which one of us has it worse honestly. You might have got off easier than I will." Lying stiff at my feet, I held nothing against him for what he said to me. On the contrary, I felt closer to him than when he was alive. Like a sieve, death filtered out his impurities and the shortcomings of our relationship. Yet I got to experience that as a result of having killed him, so I didn't regret it. Soon, the sound of heavy footsteps came from the hallway. A firm knock on the door alerted me that the time had come to say goodbye and head out into the unknown of the future, which might not be too long a journey.

"Come in," I said.

"How about locking your door at least now, huh?" Bone reproached me.

"It doesn't matter anymore. Thanks for coming."

"What happened?"

He walked around the corpse and gave me a probing, suspicious look.

"He messed up."

"What, he fucked your woman? What the hell are you doing man? Did anyone see you, did you leave any traces behind?"

"No," I answered although I had no way of knowing for certain.

"I honestly hope that's the case. Because if you're wrong, then I really shouldn't be here."

"I understand."

"I'm not sure you do; if we run into any sort of trouble, my entire life is on the line. This is not the same as our cleaning missions, that shit was organized and we only came in at the end when it was safe. But this right here, this is far from safe."

"Well, he's dead now, and you're here. Are you gonna help me or not?"

"Watch how you talk. You're lucky I answered in the first place. It's in both our interests that you don't get caught. But we're gonna have a chat about that later. I took a cab here, so go get your car and bring it in front of the entrance."

I said no more and did as he instructed. With the car downstairs, we picked up the body and carried it through the hallway. Getting to the car, Bone put down the body's legs to open the trunk, then we lifted it and placed it diagonally to make it fit. Without a word, we got in and drove to the forest. Not the one by the quarry, but the one where we'd buried the other bodies. Bone did ask me briefly on the way:

"Who is he?"

"Ritchie, my friend."

"Your friend. What did he do exactly?"

I didn't want to tell Bone what happened, nor make the effort to come up with a lie. In the end, it did not matter what I'd tell him.

"He did me wrong. It's a long story, I'd rather not go into it."

Then the rest of the drive took place in perfect silence. When we made it halfway through the forest, Bone spoke again.

"Keep going. I can't remember where we buried the others, so let's not risk digging anyone up by mistake."

Thus, we went to the other end of the forest. The trees rose tall and thin in the dark. We noticed an open space close to the right side of the tracks and stopped there.

"You do have a shovel I suppose," Bone said.

"Yeah."

"OK. I'll go first, then you take over."

I had no lantern, so we relied solely on our eyesight to dig a proper hole. The soil was cold and stiff. While Bone dug, I wondered whether I'd be able to do my part, given my dead right hand. I had no problems carrying the body because I learned to place my left hand under my right one for direction. For lifting it, I still had some strength in my right arm and could use my wrist as a lever. However, that night I had to adapt to using the shovel to do my part. Normally smoking or texting his girlfriend, Bone now watched me as I dug. He did it to survey me I thought. It wasn't clear what he'd meant by needing to have a chat once we were done, but the way I figured it could have meant any number of things.

"Work's been going well for a while," he said all of a sudden. "Steady, but good. Carrying a bunch of stuff from one place to another, we're basically just driving all day long. It's nice," he spoke lighting his customary cigarette finally.

I didn't want to entertain him, so I shut up and continued to dig. I stopped briefly to rest my wrist and wipe the sweat off my forehead.

"Anything wrong with your hand?" Bone asked.

"No, just tired."

"Aha. Honestly, I'm surprised you took it this far when things escalated between you two," he referred to me and Ritchie. "I'm surprised because I thought that's why you quit doing missions."

"I would've avoided it if I could."

"But still, these things are always avoidable. That much I know."

With the pit close to being fully dug, I sensed a weird excitement energizing me in anticipation of something. Unsure what to do next, I took out two more shovelfuls, but then Bone talked again.

"Could use another person to help us out. Initially, I thought that's why you called. I guess that would have been too convenient to be real though," he scoffed at me.

"Sorry to disappoint."

"I still haven't decided what to make of this, by the way. It leaves me in a tough position."

"What do you mean?" I asked.

"The fact you simply went on to murder someone. Not that it concerns you, but you can't even imagine how easily I can be linked to you. Even the fact you called me so shortly after you've done it can incriminate me. I actually never believed you'd turn me down, twice even. I've kinda lost a bit of trust in you since then."

"So if I came to work for you now, even after killing Ritchie, you'd trust me again?"

"It'd show me that you're committed at least. I can't explain better than this, but I'd really prefer you to work with me."

"I'm sorry, but I can't."

"OK, listen to me", he said and put out his cigarette in the dirt. "This is the last time I'm offering you the chance to join. I won't ask you again."

He sat on the edge of the pit with his knees at the same level as my head. We weren't facing each other since I'd been careful not to throw dirt on him. Also, I could not distinguish his arms from the rest of his body because of the dark. He might have been keeping one hand by the belt the entire time and I wouldn't know it. Spontaneously, with a mechanical gesture, I grabbed the gun I had on me, turned towards Bone, and shot him. The bullet must have hit his chest, although I couldn't grasp what happened. The shot took away his breath and then he fell on his back. I waited and waited for a sign of life from him, but his legs didn't move. Unsure whether he died, I dragged him towards me, half hoping that he faked it and would now shoot me in the head. I pulled him all the way down and he fell to the bottom of the pit with a thump. His head and limbs took a moment to settle into place, along the cold dirt. Then he didn't flinch anymore.

Again, numbing tiredness got into me, but I had to see it through. I threw the shovel out and climbed up with some struggle. The trees gathered around me as I walked towards the car, whose lights were turned off. There was no light around, other than the moon's glares which seeped through the forest's canopy, more like a ghostly fog than anything. With my steps sinking into the dead leaves and the mud, I opened the trunk and lifted the body out piece by piece. It didn't matter that the layers covering it were ripped up in the process, as long as I managed to drag him to the pit. Holding the feet tight, I moved backwards until the edge of the grave. There I looked at Bone one last time, but I stared too long because his facial features, vague and opaque at first, became as clear as day. The moonlight fell on his eyelids, which made it seem like his eyes were open, and stared back at me. Before it creeped me out, I rolled the corpse down. It fell over Bone's upper body, covering his face. Then already stuck between that eerie moment and the desolate future soon to come, I filled up the pit, went to the car, and drove away in a hurry.

The blackness of night began to dilute while I headed towards the town. The road led me through an open plain, with nothing but the hills of the quarry and some tall blocks in the far distance. I had nowhere to go, because nowhere could I escape myself. I'd already decided not to go back to the apartment. Even if it seemed a possibility, it wouldn't be safe for long, since I killed one of the heads of the local mob. Surely, they would have tracked me down and dealt with me accordingly. While in general it wouldn't be a bad thing, I didn't want to go that way, hunted by a bunch of callous criminals. There'd been enough trouble and heartache; all I wanted was peace.

I drove around the town for a while until the morning blue hour. Soon, the sun would rise and the quarry was a nice place to go and watch it. I drove through town, past my building and the trash can, and towards the bridge. The old man should find the envelope shortly. I liked to imagine him sharing his joy with the little girl when opening the envelope, and even with the dog.

Crossing the bridge, the water susurrated blue and clean. In a few minutes, the clearing shaped up at the horizon, as the hill with the quarry reigned over the surroundings. I stopped the car and made my way down the grassy slope overlooking the glade. There was a boulder close to where Jane, Soph, and I had our picnic. I sat there and watched the sunrise. The first rays of light caressed my face, while the fresh air filled my lungs. I wanted to breathe and let go of all the things which held me back and burdened my existence, so I began by taking off the bandage. My right hand appeared to have dried out somehow and had the color of lead, which in the meantime reached my wrist. I had to do something about that as well. There weren't many options that could make things better, however. I reached under my belt for the gun and placed it next to me. Black and ominous, it glimmered enticingly in the light. Maybe I should go for it, I thought, the time and place couldn't be more fitting.

Drawing a deep breath, the two peach trees swayed in a gentle gust of wind. They had plenty more leaves since we'd planted them, and seemed to enjoy their new home. In the remote quiet of the morning, switching my attention from one peach to the other, something in between caught my eye. Farther back in the woods, something flickered briefly and disappeared. Then I saw it again, only for a tiny glow to come out and start dancing between the trees. I watched it mesmerized and eventually it spoke to me. I didn't understand at first, but it continued talking to me until I started to get it. It was a familiar voice, whispering pleasant things in my head...

(page intentionally left blank)

Author note.

"Thank you for reading my novel Mannequin. Gaining exposure as an independent author relies mostly on word-of-mouth, so if you have the time and inclination, please consider leaving a short review wherever you can."

Yours truly,
SP

Printed in Great Britain
by Amazon